Rescued?

Emmy Hoyes

Copyright © 2024 Emmy Hoyes
All rights reserved.

All the characters in this book are fictitious,
and any resemblance to actual persons, living or dead,
is purely coincidental.

Contents

Introduction	5
Knock, Knock	7
Surplus to Requirement	21
The Chair	29
The Silent Traveller	39
Swiftwater	61
Who is a Good Doggie?	69
A Cross on Your Foot	79
What Kind of Mountain Rescuer Are You?	87
Ruby	95
Dear Diary	107
Dead Still	117
First Time	125
I Had Just	131
Bodies in the Water	133
Under Ground	141
Snowbound	149
Flip Flop, Flip Flop	157
A Tiger in the Dale	169

Off the Cliff	193
The Descent of Pot Noodle	199
Finding Funds	221
Year 2053	233
Dear Mountain Rescue…	245
Acknowledgements	251
About the Author	252

Introduction

If, like me, you hate introductions and just want to start the 'real' book, then feel free to go ahead. You can always come back and read this later. However, if you know nothing about volunteer rescue services then this introduction might be worthwhile.

The UK has hundreds of volunteer search and rescue teams that spring into action if you are cragfast on a Welsh mountain, shipwrecked off the Cornish coast, have broken your ankle in a woodland in Surrey or are stuck in quicksand in Morecambe Bay. Team members are unpaid and on standby 24 hours a day, 365 days per year. In addition to attending callouts, they dedicate time to training, kit maintenance and fundraising to cover the cost of equipment, vehicles, buildings and insurance. They rely on YOUR generosity to save lives. Please consider helping your local team so they are able to help you or your family when you need them.

Every area and terrain has its own set of unique challenges that vary in nature more than you might think. Six years as a volunteer in the Swaledale

Mountain and Cave Rescue Team provided the inspiration for these stories. While none of the events described in this book are actually true (and some frankly are outrageous) everyone one includes an element of truth.

All the characters in this book are fictitious and any resemblance to actual persons (or animals), living or dead is purely coincidental.

If you ever need help, call 999, ask for Police (or Coast Guard if you are on the coast) and then the rescue service you require, such as mountain or cave rescue.

Knock, Knock...

The sun was setting over the frozen moor, orange light reflected in the ice-covered puddles like oval mirrors scattered along the gravel track.

Gordon fumbled with the padlock to the shooting cabin, his fingers stiff from the cold. He had promised to get the old stone building warm, or at least above zero, before anyone else arrived. After removing the lock, he used his shoulder to barge the door open, stumbling into the sparsely furnished hut together with a few dried leaves trapped in the door frame. He lit some candles and placed a six-pack of beer on the dusty table. There was a fireplace, but no firewood. In the corner hung a tap above a stainless steel sink, but as he suspected, the pipes had been turned off for the winter.

It was the weekend before Christmas and time for the annual selection of new mountain rescue trainees. The applicants had been set a navigation challenge that would take them to this remote cabin long after the sun had set, provided they could read a map and cope with the freezing temperatures. It was an opportunity to weed out candidates that might look good on paper, but in real life were heroic wannabes or snowflakes. After thirty years in the team, he could spot them a mile away.

Gordon found the old gas heater hidden under a couple of musty blankets, cursing that yet again he'd forgotten to service it. It had been a bastard to light last time. He brushed a layer of cobwebs off the heating element and rocked the gas bottle back and forth - at least there was plenty of gas left. Half a box of matches later, a pathetic orange flame danced across the front of the heater and the cabin filled with the smell of burning dust.

Gordon cracked open a beer and sat down on a wooden chair in front of the heater. The beer was cold and the heat from the fire massaged his face. He leaned back on the chair, crossed his arms over his belly and closed his eyes.

Knock, knock, knock...

He wasn't sure how long he'd been sleeping, but the sun had set and the only light came from the heater and the candles on the table. He opened the door letting in a blast of cold air. In the dark stood three imposing figures, each holding a package. Not the typical outdoor types wearing Gore-Tex and head torches. Instead, they were dressed in elaborate crowns and heavy cloaks embroidered with golden thread.

'Recruits?' he asked, wondering if the invite had specified fancy dress.

The men murmured among themselves. One of them pointed to the sky causing more mumbling.

'Come in, will you?' Gordon said. 'We can't have all the heat escaping.'

Once inside, the three men scanned the room, their eyes darting from corner to corner. Gordon hoped they had brought beer, or at least some snacks, but the boxes they were carrying weren't large enough and looked far too fancy.

'We've come from the East,' the man, dressed in red, announced.

'Yes, that's right. You will have set off from Reeth.'

'Gentlemen,' said the man in green while shaking his head. 'I don't think this is the right place.'

'No, it is,' Gordon said to make them feel more at ease. 'You've passed the navigational challenge. I can show you on the map.'

'We don't need a map,' said the third man, whose cloak was deep blue with a satin brocade. 'We're following a star.'

Gordon rubbed his chin. Was this a New Age thing? Or were they ex-navy and more used to celestial navigation?

The men whispered to each other and, without further ado, departed into the freezing winter night. Gordon watched their silhouettes disappear into the darkness before closing the door.

The Magi? Surely not. Neither his radio set nor mobile phone worked out here, or he could have checked whether the three men had been asked to act as casualties for the recruits to encounter along the way. Maybe they had strayed onto the moor after a nativity play in one of the village halls?

Gordon returned to his chair and let out a sigh. Pressure was building behind his eyes. Maybe he was coming down with a cold. He hadn't long sat down when the door flew open.

'Yarrrr, matey!' shouted a vibrant character standing in the doorway. 'Long John Silver at your service.'

Gordon rubbed his eyes at the sight of the one-legged man with long black hair and pirate hat who was supporting himself on a tall wooden crutch.

'It's the right place, isn't it? I've passed the navigational test, haven't I? You must be expecting me, yes?' The pirate barged into the hut, pushing Gordon aside. 'I'm the first! Arrrrr!'

Gordon remembered a 'John Silver' on the list of names he'd been given. So far everything made sense, which was more than he could have said about the previous visitors. 'What about your partner? You're supposed to navigate as a pair?'

The pirate smiled and pointed to the green parrot sitting on his shoulder. 'Meet Captain Flint. She has also applied to join the team.'

'I'm not sure we accept parrots as...' Gordon started.

'Flint - let's hear it!'

Figure of eight, figure of eight, ka, ka, ka, figure of eight!

'See! She's been practising her knots.' Long John pulled out a chair, sat down at the table and helped himself to one of Gordon's beers. He emptied half the can into his mouth and let out a reverberating burp. 'I'm an expert at rope work, navigation and pillaging, arrr! But I know what you're thinking.' He held his hand up to stop Gordon from interrupting. 'How can a one-legged man carry a stretcher? Rest assured, I have done much harder things in my life. You even suggesting it might be a problem would be a pure sign of ableist prejudice.'

Gordon hadn't even thought that far. Truth be told, he was more worried about what the man was capable of, instead of what he wasn't able to do. He was also starting to feel queasy. When he turned his head, his eyes seemed to take a second or so to catch up.

Knock, knock, knock...

Gordon drew a deep breath before answering the door. His jaw dropped at the sight of a young woman wearing a turquoise t-shirt stretched across a torso that managed to be slim and round, at the same time as being muscular. Her shapely buttocks were contained in the tightest, shortest pants he'd ever seen. So tight that there was no room for pockets, instead holsters containing handguns were strapped to her tanned athletic thighs. Wait! Guns? He looked at her face.

'I'm Lara. Lara Croft.'

Gordon blushed. It was a dream come true. 'Come in!'

She brushed past him, a long auburn plait swinging behind her. A waft of wood resin and beeswax mixed with fresh female sweat reached his nose making his knees weak. He looked around to try and spot her team mate before closing the door.

Her face stiffened when she saw John at the table. 'So I'm only second...'

Gordon imagined having Lara on the team. Her powerful moves helping them rig ropes for extreme stretcher handling, huddling close beside her while administering first aid to casualties or getting changed after swiftwater training on the banks of the River Swale.

'Sorry, I've got to ask. Your teammate?'

'Oh, him. He was slowing me down. You wouldn't want him in your team, trust me. You'll find him in Rowleth Woods. Don't worry, he didn't suffer.' Lara patted one of her guns.

Gordon was lost for words. He stared at her ample chest while wondering if there was any way he could un-hear what she'd just told him, or frame it differently to make it sound more palatable.

'I'm going for a slash…' John stood up knocking his chair over. He waved a hand in front of Gordon's face as he passed, but failed to get a reaction.

'So,' Lara asked, 'do I get a place on the team?'

Gordon rubbed his face. His mind said one thing, his heart another. He drew a deep breath trying to balance Lara's skill set against the fact that she wasn't a team player.

'Come on,' she said, putting her hands on her hips. 'I can't wait all night. I'm off to Egypt tomorrow, then Peru.'

'How much time do you spend in Swaledale?' he asked, realising there might be an even bigger issue at stake. 'If a team member isn't available to deploy at the drop of a hat, it doesn't matter how capable they are. Their skills are of no use to the team.' Gordon sadly knew what her answer would be and smiled apologetically.

'Suit yourself,' Lara replied and left as suddenly as she had appeared, slamming the door behind her.

Gordon dropped his head in disappointment even though he knew he'd made the right decision. He returned on unsteady legs to the chair in front of the heater and noticed that John had made off with his beers.

Just as he got comfortable, there was another knock on the door. He found himself swaying first to the right and then to the left as he went to open it. Perhaps he'd drunk those beers himself but forgotten about it?

To Gordon's surprise, the ground was covered in a thick layer of snow. There was also a large man standing by the door. At least this candidate looked suitably dressed for the winter weather in a red stocking cap and a big red woolly coat. A pristine white beard finished the cosy-looking outfit.

'Ho! Ho! Ho!' the man greeted him.

'Father Christmas! Come inside,' Gordon said, surprised that he wasn't surprised.

'I've tied my sleigh to the fence post over there, is that…'

'That's perfect!' Gordon's heart did a jump for joy. The real Father Christmas! It must be. Look at all those reindeer!

The bearded man brushed the snow off his coat and followed Gordon inside.

'Please, take a seat.' Gordon offered him the chair in front of the heater. 'Unfortunately I've got nothing in the way of food or drink to offer you.'

'That's perfectly fine,' Father Christmas replied. 'I'm on my pre-Christmas diet anyway.'

'I can't tell you how chuffed I am that you want to join our mountain rescue team.'

'Oh well. As you'll know I have 364 days off every year and even though I'm old, I feel I have more to offer.'

Gordon nodded, excited about putting together a Christmas wishlist for the team.

'And I don't mind using my reindeer to help with the transport of casualties. We fly even in the most challenging conditions.'

Gordon couldn't believe his ears. The team would have its own air ambulance! One that was far more robust than the helicopters that they often requested when casualties were far from a road or seriously injured. He couldn't wait to tell the rest of the team about his new recruit.

'Can I take some personal details for the membership form?' Gordon asked, not wanting to waste a minute. 'Gender. Profession. Address? North Pole, I presume?'

'I have a second home in Keld if that looks better on the application,' Father Christmas suggested.

Gordon nodded. 'Age?'

'1741.'

'Years?'

'Of course it's years.' Father Christmas chuckled.

'Oh, okay.' Gordon estimated that it would push up the average age of a team member to 97 years. He scratched his head before writing '65 years' on the form. Nobody was going to check.

'I just have one more question. Were you assigned a partner for this exercise?' Gordon held his breath hoping Father Christmas wasn't going to break his already dented heart.

'Oh yes. Mr Alek. He refused to get in my sleigh. Said he'd take the track here rather than fly. I'm very sorry. I'm sure he'll be here any minute now.'

Donk, donk, doingk...

'That's probably him then,' Gordon said and went to the door. It was considerably heavier than last time and the hinges were creaking like they hadn't been greased for a century. Stuck to the outside of the door, via some sort of sink plunger, was a human-sized pepper-pot-shaped robot. A single eyestalk swizzled around to face him.

'*Exterminate...*' sounded an electronic voice.

'No,' Gordon said firmly and locked the door shut. 'Can you believe the audacity...' He turned expecting to see Father Christmas but the room was empty. A few flakes of soot fell from the chimney by the fireplace. 'Ah well, it was probably too good to be true.'

Gordon plonked himself down in the chair. The room was spinning. All he wanted to do was sleep.

Knock, knock...

Gordon sighed. Not again. He was tempted to ignore it. Even standing up seemed like too much effort. But yet again, he dragged himself to the door.

'Gordie?'

'Dad?' Gordon knew it couldn't be his father standing outside the door. But there he was, the same heavy eyebrows, the bulbous nose and the double chin. It was like facing a mirror.

'Room for an old one on the team?'

His dad would have been the perfect mountain rescuer with his knowledge of the area and no-problem-is-too-big attitude. Having worked as a paramedic, his casualty care would have been spot on. There was only one problem, Gordon buried him ten years ago.

His father tilted his head and studied Gordon's eyes. 'You're not feeling so good, are you?'

The nausea was coming in waves from his stomach up to his throat. 'No, no. I'm fine.' Gordon felt his father's arm around his shoulder, turning him away from the warmth of the cabin, towards the coldness of the winter night. 'No Dad, let's go inside. I haven't even got my coat on.' Gordon spun around to see a tall thin figure draped in a black cloak surrounded by a cloud of sweet-smelling ash standing by his father's side. The large hood covered the man's face. Gordon wasn't an idiot, he knew who it was.

'You paired up with Death?' he said.

His father shrugged. 'No choice, I'm afraid.'

Death beckoned with a bony finger for Gordon to follow him.

'Is this it?' He looked at his dad who had pity written across his face.

Gordon's willpower faded. He glanced into the cabin just as the last candle on the table burnt out, leaving the room in darkness. He took his father's outstretched hand and stepped into the deep snow surprised that he didn't feel the cold.

'Hey, wake up!'

Gordon felt a slap across his cheek and his head throbbed to the rhythm of his heartbeat.

'Welcome back. We thought we'd lost you,' Gary said, helping him sit up in the snow outside the cabin. Gordon rubbed his neck and drew deep breaths of fresh air surrounded by team members, all shining their head torches at his tender eyes. His brain was booting up again.

'The heater is off now. I've opened all the windows. The carbon monoxide should be gone in a few minutes,' Keith announced. 'We can leave if Gordon's up to it.'

'Where are we going?' Gordon asked. He stood up and bent over for a few seconds to let his blood pressure catch up. It felt like he'd come back from a long holiday and the world had moved on without him.

'We've got a callout, so the selection night has been postponed.' Neil opened the rear door of the team's Land Rover to let Gordon climb inside. He was joined by a team member on either side. The engine roared to life and the headlights lit up a magical landscape draped in freshly fallen snow. Gordon leaned forward to get a better look. Surely, those weren't sleigh marks, were they?

'An ambulance assist,' Neil continued. 'They're struggling to get to a woman who has given birth in her car. It's stuck in a snowdrift on a track across from Arkengarthdale, but we don't know where.'

Something stirred inside Gordon, a warm feeling spreading through his chest. 'Just follow that star,' he said and pointed to a bright dot in the sky.

Surplus to Requirement

I put my head inside the small tent and smell piss and alcohol. A man, curled up inside, lifts his head in response to the bright light from my head torch. He recoils in fear, then grimaces. He brings an unsteady hand up to shield his eyes, the other is wrapped around a bottle of whisky. Co-op's own brand.

'Are you Martin Brough?' I ask. He matches the description: 59, balding, dark jacket and jeans. He doesn't look like a hiker who's camping in the middle of a grouse moor for pleasure.

I get my radio out and leave him inside the tent.

'Rescue-Control from Rescue-Colin, priority message.' The handset beeps but I get no response. 'Any call sign from Rescue-Colin, misper found, please respond.' Where the hell is everyone?

I push the tent flap to one side as a strong gust catches an empty tablet box. I follow it with my torch as it bounces across the moorland. It's briefly stuck on a tussock, but soon tumbles on and is lost to the darkness.

'What have you taken?'

'Ye've no frickin' right to interfere! It's my choice, nothin' to do with you,' the man rants.

'Have you taken some tablets?'

'None of yer business. Leave me alone.'

After another failed attempt with the radio, I look across the dark hills, but can't see any lights. My sweat-soaked base layer offers no protection against the cold, so I dive inside the tent to get out of the wind.

'What was in that box?'

He's lying with his back to me. I lean over for a closer look, but the fucker turns and swings his fist in my direction. I lunge forward and pin him to the ground, my legs either side of his body, my hands on his arms. His red eyes are bulging while he's trying to free himself.

'I'm allowed to kill myself. Ye can't stop me,' he shouts and spits at me. His gob lands on his own chin.

'You idiot,' I shout. 'It's fucking Christmas Day. I could have been home having dinner with my family. But no, I've had to walk in the wind and rain for nine hours looking for you, you wanker.'

He stares at me, his face hard to read. When he speaks I'm hit by whisky fumes and tooth decay. 'At least ye've got a job. And I'm sure ye get paid extra. Christmas and all. Cash to spend on yer missus–'

I lean forward and growl in his face, 'I'm always on call. Every fucking minute of every fucking day. And you know what? I don't get any money whatsoever. I'm a volunteer.'

He spots the fabric badge on my sleeve.

'Bloody Mountain Rescue. Hell, that's bloody brilliant. Now ye can go home and brag about how amazing ye are and how ye've saved a life, ye smug bastard. Thing is, I don't wanna be saved.'

I lift his torso by his jacket and pull him close. 'Then maybe you should have done a better job, matey, because you went missing twenty-four hours ago and you're still alive. Pretty piss poor, if you ask me.'

I let go. His body goes limp but his face stiffens. I slide off him as he rolls over and pukes. There's a cluster of white tablets in the vomit.

I gag and crawl out of the tent. Deep breaths. I sit down, head between my legs. What the fuck is going on with me? I need to save the batteries, so turn the torch off. Darkness creeps into every crevice. Stars appear overhead, first just a few, then hundreds, and after a minute there are millions of twinkling lights forming the Milky Way. I'm insignificant and it gives me comfort. Should I leave him? It's what he deserves. I get up and put my backpack on.

'Sorry... I said, I'm sorry,' he shouts from inside the tent. He wriggles out to join me. 'Just wanted to punish my missus. Bloody Christmas Day of all days... I'm such an eejit. Those tablets, they're only ibuprofens.'

He sits down on the soft heather with his head in his hands. After a minute, I join him.

'Hey, come on, say summat. I'm apologising here. I'll even apologise to yer wife if ye want me to.' The man bumps my shoulder with drunken impatience like he's my mate.

'We're divorced,' I confess.

'But ye're on good terms, right? If ye still celebrate Christmas together.'

'No, I made that up. Katie won't even let me see the boys.'

'That's arse. Never had kids, me. Had plenty of wives though. On my fourth. Doesn't get any easier. How old?'

'Six and eight,' I reply.

The man offers me his whisky. I unscrew the top and let a mouthful burn its way down into my empty stomach.

'Why did you stop here? It's miles from anywhere.'

'Don't know, just kept walking. Totally blootered. Hoped to just keel over if I pushed hard enough. Haven't got a bloody clue where I am.'

'Why'd you want to do it?' I take another sip of the whisky. It's harsh but warming.

'I dunno.'

We sit in silence. The moon is a thin sliver and gives just enough light to make out where the hills meet the sky.

'I was made redundant. Thirty fucking years, six more until retirement,' he says and sighs.

'What did you do?' I don't care but ask anyway.

'Glass blower. University of Glasgow, Chemistry Department. Bloody good too. Last one in the country. Rare as rocking horse shit. If I'd been a tree, I'd have a bloody preservation order on me. Not surplus to requirement. Same words my missus used.'

'Did she really?'

'Nae. But she might as well have. Said she wanted me gone. So, I thought, 'Sure, I'll go.''

I hand the bottle back. The man keeps talking. About his work, his parents but mostly about his wife. He doesn't seek any input from me so my attention wanes.

He waves his hand in front of my face. 'What were you doing then, when you got the call?'

I don't tell him that I'd been sitting in my dining room, tasting the metal and grease from a shotgun barrel in my mouth, my thumb resting on the trigger. Two envelopes on the table, one for my mum and one for my boys. I'd tried to write one for Katie too, but failed.

I won't tell him that when the text message came through I thought it was her, sensing what I was about to do, lending me some hope. Letting me have the boys for Easter or just checking on me. But of course, it hadn't been, it was only a search for yet another despondent 'misper'. I had thrown the phone against the wall and put my thumb back on the trigger.

I shan't tell him that Katie had left me the previous Christmas, saying how she couldn't stand it anymore, never knowing if I was going to be there or not. Always abandoning her and the boys to rush off on rescues, searches and training sessions. Always prioritising other people over my own family, for the glory, she'd called it. Anyway, it was over and she'd found someone else, an accountant in Kent, five hundred miles away. And worst of all, the boys loved him.

I can't tell him that I'd tossed the gun to the floor and set off determined to kill the guy who wants forty people to abandon their Christmas celebrations to spend the day trailing across the moors because he happens to feel a bit low that day.

I tell him, 'Nothing much.'

'So I saved you from a dull Christmas then?' He hands me the bottle again. There's not much left, so I finish it off.

'I suppose you could say that,' I say and look at the sky. I'm willing a star to fall, but they keep clinging on. Just like every fucking sad bastard on this fucked up planet.

The radio buzzes into life. 'Rescue-Colin from Rescue-Control.'

I fumble in my coat for the mic. 'Rescue-Control from Rescue-Colin. Pass your message.'

'Your search party has reported you missing. Is everything OK? Over.'

'Yes, Yes. I've located the misper. Over.'

'Great. What's his status? We have heli-med on stand-by. Over.'

I look at Martin. 'You're alright, aren't you?'

He nods, then adds, 'I'll be fine. As long as ye know the way off this bloody hill. Don't want to get lost and have to call frickin' Mountain Rescue to find us.' He laughs at his own joke.

I can't help but smile and I press the microphone button. 'No heli-med required. We will start moving down to the track at Yellow Moss Burn. If you can have a vehicle waiting for us that would be great. Rescue-Colin to stand by.'

'Sorry to give ye more hassle, but I probably need a lift home. Pretty sure I'm over the limit,' he says.

'Don't worry. We'll figure something out.'

We pull the tent down and gather up the empty bottles before we head off. I notice the search parties on the surrounding hillsides, all returning to control, their torch lights darting across the lumpy moor. They hope to get back to their families in time to have some leftover Christmas dinner, watch their kids play with their presents and enjoy a glass of port with their partner. A team vehicle weaves its way along the valley bottom in our direction, blue lights flashing.

'You know what,' I say to Martin. 'Why don't you come home with me? I don't think you should be on your own tonight.'

The Chair

Gordon winds down the passenger window when he sees spindly young Tom waiting at the bus stop. He's the newest member of the mountain rescue team.

'Want a lift?'

'Oh yeah! Seems the bus is a no-show today.'

Gordon had reservations about taking on a member who didn't have their own transport. 'Widen the scope,' Sarah, the training officer, had told him. 'Young people these days can't afford a car. It shouldn't prevent them from joining the team.' To Gordon, not willingly owning a car was just a way of avoiding your turn to drive to the pub.

'I'm excited about tonight's committee meeting. You know, to see what goes on in the background,' Tom says as he gets into the Skoda and fights with the seatbelt that refuses to unspool for him.

Gordon grunts. Until eight months ago, subterfuge had been the only way to make sure every committee post was filled. Now members are asked to attend at least one meeting to encourage them to take on further roles, a strategy that so far hasn't yielded a single new addition to the team's committee. This evening, it's Tom's turn.

'It's not that exciting,' Gordon says in an attempt to lower Tom's expectations.

'But you're the Chair, right?'

Gordon nods. He remembers the last Annual General Meeting when, half way through, he'd gone to relieve himself. When he returned, the committee had proposed, seconded and voted him in as Chair. Still, only a month to go until the next AGM, and this time he wasn't going to leave the room.

'Anything interesting on the agenda?' Tom chirps.

'No.'

It is the same agenda every month. The same things are said by the same people, and he often wonders why they couldn't just copy the minutes from the last meeting and change the date. Then he remembers about 'Any Other Business' and shudders. That's the time when he holds his breath, wondering how quickly he can declare the meeting finished. Never quick enough, it turns out. There's always someone who wants to throw the cat amongst the pigeons, who feels the need to officially address something that could be sorted quietly, like in the old days, before everything needed to be discussed and documented. Gordon was the first to admit that he was turning into more of a dinosaur with every passing day.

Gordon enters the training room as everyone is arranging chairs into a semi-circle. Stu hands him the agenda.

Stu's in his ninth year as secretary. He never turns up to training or callouts but does look good in a red uniform, and he's not bad at taking notes. Bumping him off the team for non-compliance is not even worth thinking about. If anyone suggests it, it certainly won't make the minutes.

When Gordon starts the meeting, twelve people are facing him and only Tom sports an enthusiastic smile.

'Okay. Apologies for running over by three hours last time. First up, minutes from the last meeting. Any objections?' Quick glance confirms that nobody in the room has bothered to read them. 'Excellent. Next item, summary of callouts in the last month. Over to you Neil.'

Neil is what the team calls a 'great asset'. He has the knack of always being available, keen to pass on his extensive skills and what's more amazing, everyone likes him. He starts reading from a piece of paper. 'April saw an average number of callouts. The usual lower leg injuries, one above Shin Cliff and the other in Steep Fall Woods. Then we had the crag-fast sheep up near Eweno Weir and the day after we fished a spaniel out of a sinkhole near Woof pot. The only other incident that's worth mentioning is the missing Duke of Edinburgh group last Saturday evening, four sixteen-year-old lads, three hours overdue.'

People shuffle nervously in their seats.

'We were lucky Jim found them in the pub. However, only ten team members responded that they were available to attend the search. Of them, only three felt sober enough to drive and the others were asking for lifts. I can't organise taxis, as well as running control. It's great that people are careful when it comes to drink driving, especially after the police breathalysed the whole team on the early morning callout on New Year's Day. Just wonder how we can avoid this being a regular occurrence?'

Gordon scans the faces of the committee members. The room is deathly quiet. Tom sticks his hand eagerly in the air.

'Yes, Tom?'

'We could organise a rota system where people promise to not have a drink on certain days?'

Gordon closes his eyes and breathes out slowly to quench a sigh. 'Anyone wants to add anything?' he asks, but everyone's staring at the floor. He's about to whisper to Stu not to record Tom's suggestion, but the look on Stu's face says he hasn't even registered Neil's concerns in the first place.

He's about to move on to the next item on the agenda when Tom interrupts. 'I don't know why you are all so obsessed with alcohol. I don't feel the need to drink at all.'

Jim looks at him with his saggy eyes resting above his droopy purple nose. He's a so-called super-user, or more fashionably put, a functioning alcoholic. 'Hey son, that's excellent news, although if I may say so, a total waste since you don't even drive.'

'Let's move on to membership updates,' Gordon interrupts. 'Gary, over to you.'

Gary stands up like he's about to deliver a speech. 'In this period, we've had three new enquiries about joining the team. All seem like promising candidates, so I've put them on the waiting list.'

Gary sits down again while Gordon scans the bored faces that line the walls of the training room. There's one person who's waving his hand above his head.

'Tom, you want to add something?'

'Yes, I just wonder if any of the applicants aren't of white British heritage. I can't be the only one who's concerned that the team isn't diverse enough?'

Gary stands up again. 'Of course we care about diversity, but we haven't had anyone diverse apply yet.'

'Then maybe we should encourage applicants from other backgrounds by promoting the team as more inclusive,' Tom says.

'Hang on son,' Jim wades in. 'You might not have noticed, being colour blind and all that, but our patch has almost no diverse people in it, of any kind. Unless you want to start recruiting from Darlington and Middlesbrough, which never mind the travel times, would be breaking the rules as they are covered by other rescue teams.'

'I'm just saying…'

'If you're insinuating that our team is deliberately trying to avoid being diverse you can wind your neck in. To prove it, I'm proud to say that I'm half Irish.'

There's nothing like a good argument to wake people up. Committee members now sit up straight, ready to enter the battle. Only Stu is leaning back on his chair, spinning his pen between his fingers, waiting to see who comes out on top. It's less hassle to write the minutes from the winner's perspective.

'There're many ways of being diverse,' Tom says. 'What about encouraging the LGBTQ community to apply to the team. Do you even collect information about this?'

Gary looks at Gordon for support, but he remains silent. 'No, we don't. I'm not sure it would give people the right impression if we asked them for their sexual preferences when joining the team. Although, we might have members who are diverse already, without us knowing?'

Everyone looks at Stu.

'Hey, why are you all staring at me?'

Gordon intervenes. 'Folks, calm down. Let's agree, for the record, that we all would like to see a more diverse team. Though we're not yet diverse, I would like to think we're inclusive. Jim here is a good example of that.'

People snigger.

Sarah holds her hand up.

'Yes, Sarah?'

'We only have four women on the team. Last time I looked there wasn't a shortage of women in our area.'

'Thanks for making that valid point, but due to the many items left on the agenda, I regret that we have to move on to more pressing matters. Next up, bobble hats.' Gordon leans in Stu's direction. 'I thought we discussed this last time?'

'We did,' Stu points to the minutes. 'We decided against a bobble on the new hats because they wouldn't fit underneath our helmets.'

'So?'

'Craig asked if we could discuss the possibility of having a removable bobble.'

Gordon shakes his head in despair. 'The answer is no. Next item: equipment grant. Five thousand pounds to spend on new technology to modernise mountain rescue. Suggestions anyone?'

'Removable bobbles?' Jim mumbles.

Gordon already knows who's going to say what. Keith is going to argue that the team should invest in jetpacks. Jim wants the search dogs to be issued with bottles of brandy. Stu wants a sauna built at the depot, but is trying to disguise it as a drying room for the swiftwater rescue suits. The only reasonable request has come from Sarah. She wants the team to invest in a digital learning platform so that members can learn more medical skills, but the last time it was discussed, it ended up being a fight with people saying the team would be better off with a selection of YouTube videos and didn't need to spend thousands on software since everyone knows software should be free.

'Any suggestions, apart from the usual ones?' Gordon clarifies and Keith, Stu, Jim and Sarah put their hands down. Only Tom still has his raised.

'Tom, what useful nugget of wisdom would you like to impart on the team, considering you've only just joined and aren't a member of the committee?'

To Gordon's amazement, Tom starts to speak, undeterred or perhaps unaware of the sarcasm in his last question. 'I was wondering if maybe we could look into buying a drone? It could help with searches.'

Gordon looks around the room. People are nodding their support and more importantly, nobody is objecting. 'Excellent. Tom, speak to Keith, our equipment officer and make sure you have a proposal ready for the next meeting.' Gordon glances at Stu who confirms he's recorded this rare moment of unity amongst the committee members. 'Okay, Any Other Business? Or shall we wrap up–'

'I've got something,' Keith says and starts talking about inspection schedules for the aluminium stretchers for the next twenty minutes. Followed by Sarah, who suggests that the toilets at the base ought to have the walls repainted, triggering a half hour debate about what colour they should be. Just as it looks possible to finish the meeting, Jim requests funds for costumes for the pantomime the team is putting together to raise money for a new vehicle. It turns out that half the committee thinks the team is going to perform Cinderella while the other half is certain they'd decided on Jack and the Beanstalk. A barrel of worms is reopened that was last closed two meetings ago. While people are arguing between themselves, Gordon looks at Stu, and then at his watch. Stu gives him a nod and they get up and leave the room, switching the lights off in the process.

Tom catches up with him in the car park. 'I've missed the last bus back, any chance I could get a lift home?'

Gordon nods. 'Get in.'

'That was a really good meeting,' Tom says, again struggling to get the seatbelt to cooperate.

'You think so?'

'Yeah! Are there any posts vacant for next year?'

'I'll let you in on a secret. I'm not standing for Chair again, so if you like, I'll nominate you for the position?' Gordon smiles and starts the engine.

'Would you really? That would be amazing! Thank you so much. Fingers crossed no one else wants it.'

Gordon pulls out of the car park and rolls his eyes. 'Fingers crossed…'

The Silent Traveller

Police sirens blare out from my phone on the bedside table. It's an audible punch in the gut, a custom alert linked to a callout message to make sure I wake up. This time it's a missing walker, male in his 70s, on the Coast to Coast route.

A glance at the window confirms a mere hint of dawn, like the sun is thinking about rising, but hasn't made up its mind yet. I can't see what the weather is doing, but assume it's going to be wet, cold, and windy. It always is. Only someone who likes to suffer would walk the Coast to Coast in the middle of winter. Well, they're undoubtedly suffering now. And soon I will be too.

'Off to pay back to the community?' Sally grunts. Her eyes remain shut.

'Mmmm,' I say and stumble out of the warm bed.

'Enjoy.' Sally turns over and pulls the duvet over her head.

We retired early from teaching and bought a cottage in a quaint village in the Yorkshire Dales. I'd lie if I said I didn't feel guilty. We aren't the young blood the ageing population needs to keep the school open; we're not going to be labouring on the local farms and we probably outbid a local person hoping to get on the housing ladder. Giving something back to the community is a way of soothing the bad conscience simmering just under our skin.

Sally joined a litter-picking group and volunteers in the Save Yorkshire's Dogs charity shop every Tuesday to pay off her guilt. I thought mountain rescue sounded exciting and wasn't put off by the waiting list to join the team. That said, I don't feel quite so keen on giving something back at six o'clock on a Saturday morning in December, after wholeheartedly supporting the local pub the night before.

I rummage in my drawers, searching for base layers, fleeces, socks and waterproof trousers. In the end, I resort to scooping up an armful of clothing to take to the bathroom to avoid disturbing Sally further. After four years in the team, you'd think I'd have a bag packed for a situation like this.

Another message comes through while I'm in the kitchen making a couple of jam sandwiches, one to eat now and one to save for later. We are to rendezvous outside Keld Village Hall at eight thirty. He must have been missing for a while then if we can afford an hour getting our stuff together. I change my approach and throw a couple of eggs and some bacon in a pan. It will settle my stomach and soak up any alcohol that might still be sloshing about in my system. That, and lots of coffee.

Twenty minutes later, I arrive in Keld, the sleepy village that has looked the same for centuries; a handful of stone cottages, a village hall, a chapel on the hill. This morning it's unrecognisable, full of colourful cars with blue lights still flashing, three police vans, two mountain rescue Land Rovers, and our incident control vehicle that has all the communications and computer equipment needed to organise a thorough search. Team members pour in from all directions, bleary-eyed after a heavy Friday night. The search dogs are the first to be tasked - at least they are fully awake - even though their handlers might not be.

'Everyone's attention please,' Neil shouts. He's had specialist training and has read the book of missing person statistics. Searching is predominantly about ticking off the places that they're likely to be, until they're found, or the odds of finding them become infinitely small. 'We have a seventy-five-year-old male. Hans Lolland, an experienced walker, doing the Coast to Coast. Was last seen yesterday morning leaving Keld. His bags were picked up by the baggage transfer company and dropped off in Reeth at the Woolly Lamb Guest House in the afternoon. The owner phoned the police in the early hours of this morning when he hadn't arrived. According to the B&B in Keld, he was wearing a brown coat, a small black backpack and a dark grey hat.'

'Sounds like he doesn't want to be found,' Jim mutters before licking the edge of a cigarette paper and rolling it up around a bundle of tobacco strands.

Neil ignores him and continues. 'The police say his phone connected to a mast at three o'clock on Thursday, nothing since then. However, since there's no signal here, that's not unusual. It all points to him being somewhere on the moor between here and Reeth.' Neil gathers a bunch of paper printouts of the maps with various routes highlighted and looks across the group until he spots me. 'Gary, you can lead search team one. Jim and Jenny, you go with him. This section is yours.' He hands me a map and I wave my group over to one side.

Jenny bounces across like a keen puppy. It's her first proper search, having just become a fully qualified team member. Jim finishes his cigarette, coughs and puts his sheepskin gloves back on. He's in his seventies and nobody knows why he's still alive. Despite the quantity of beer he drinks, he looks desiccated and his clothes hang off him like from a wire hanger. One of the dog handlers once told him to cover his bare legs in case his dog thought they were dried beef tendons.

'So Gary, what's the plan?' Jim asks.

He's been in the team for thirty years, so I don't feel entirely comfortable being in charge.

'It's a hasty search so we'll follow the Coast to Coast route and keep our eyes open for anything we might find,' I reply.

'We won't see much, that's for sure.'

Jim's right. A thick mist has risen from the nearby fields or the clouds have dropped from the sky, impossible to tell which. At best, we can see ten metres ahead. We turn our radios on and leave the village via a small track that leads to the fell.

'Let's hope we find this one,' Jim mumbles.

'What do you mean?' Jenny asks.

'We had another fella, old like, also went missing. Four years ago.'

It takes a while for me to remember it. I was new then and a holiday to Florence prevented me from attending more than the first day. 'He never turned up, did he?'

'No, we searched for a week. People said he'd probably run off with a prostitute from Middlesbrough. He certainly wasn't between Keld and Reeth, I can tell you that.'

The track we're on descends toward a pretty stone bridge that takes us across the River Swale. On the other side, the path starts climbing towards the moor. I can hear Jim's chest wheeze but he's keeping up okay.

'And twenty years ago, there was another chap. Just the same,' he squeezes out, making us stop and turn around.

'With a prostitute?' Jenny asks.

'No. Or maybe. We didn't find him either.'

'Thousands of hikers walk this section every year so you're bound to lose a few,' I say. It's meant as a joke but I get no laughs.

The last steep rise of the track brings us up to the moor. We've left the fog behind and orange sunlight bounces from the dew stuck to the heather and the tall tufts of grass that line the sides of the path. The valley below is still thick with mist like the clouds have lost their buoyancy and got trapped at ground level.

'Whoa! This is amazing!' Jenny fumbles to get her phone out to take a photo.

I press the button on my radio after catching my breath.

'Rescue-Control, Rescue-Control from Rescue-One. Radio check.'

'Rescue-One. Receiving loud and clear.'

'Rescue-Control from Rescue-One, we're at the top of the track, about to head off across the moor. It's glorious up here, proper cloud inversion. Excellent visibility. Over.'

'Rescue-One, from Rescue-Control. Great news. You enjoy yourself. Let us know when you've got to the Old Gang Mine and we'll send a vehicle to pick you up. Over.'

'Yes, yes. Will do. Rescue-One to standby.'

We try to keep focused on the track and the surrounding area as we stroll off, but it's a challenge. The sky is so blue and the horizon is dotted with the tops of the surrounding hills sticking out of a sea of soft clouds.

It takes another hour to get to the end of the route and we've met a handful of walkers coming the other way. None of them have seen a man matching Hans' description. When we get to the end a Land Rover is already parked up waiting for us.

'Found anything?' Sharon asks as soon as we get close enough.

I shake my head. 'Not a thing.'

'Get in, we're starting the line searches while the weather is good.'

We get back to Keld in time for another briefing.

'Here's a photo of our misper.' Neil hands out a sheet of A4 which gets passed on from team member to team member.

'What's a misper?' Jenny whispers.

'Short for missing person,' I reply as I get handed the piece of paper. It shows an older gentleman, thin-haired, narrow-faced, wearing metal-rimmed glasses that are too big for him. He's smiling, showing his uneven teeth and a receding gumline while holding up a pint of lager to the camera as if he's toasting us. I pass it to Jenny. She looks at it with sad eyes. I remind myself that she's new, and likely to be more emotionally involved in what is happening. It will pass. It always does. Well, almost always.

'The police have enquired at the pubs and shops all down the valley–'

'All four of them?' Jim interrupts Neil since he can't resist poking fun at authorities.

'There're no sightings, so we're still working on the assumption he's somewhere up on the moor. Swale-One hasn't found anything on the route itself.' Neil throws a glance my way and I nod in agreement.

The map on the whiteboard has been divided into uneven squares marked with letters. Area A is roughly two kilometres across and borders the path which we have just walked. It has an x marked in the southeast corner, which is where Neil points.

'One of the search dogs has indicated here, so we'll start a line search coming from the east along this track, working our way to the boundary fence.'

I'd like to think we would have spotted him if he'd been walking around up there; the visibility was perfect, and on the moor there are no trees or even a bush to hide behind. Neil doesn't say it outright, but I assume we are looking for someone who is lying on the ground. Injured or dead, the heather could easily hide you.

'The police are sending a search helicopter and a drone team as soon as they become available. We're also calling in help from the neighbouring rescue teams. Numbers to be confirmed this afternoon.'

Half an hour later, I'm one of twelve team members standing on a track facing the heather-covered moor. We're side by side, ten metres apart. The sun has disappeared behind a continuous layer of thick cloud cover, taking the warming light with it. In the distance, the grey sky joins the hills with soft grey brushstrokes showing that rain is heading our way. My face already hurts from the harsh westerly wind.

Jenny is on my left, holding a bunch of yellow flags to mark the edge of the search area at regular intervals. She smiles nervously. Sharon shouts for us to start walking. With the first step, my boot sinks into deep peat and my sock soaks up cold brown water. I shudder and curse. The terrain up here is a lottery. I have to keep going to maintain a straight line and find I'm spending more time deciding where to put my feet than actually searching. After a few stops to allow people to catch up, we reach the fence line. The only find I've made is a deflated pink helium balloon.

We take up new positions along the fence to comb the next stretch of moorland. Jenny keeps her line, preventing a gap between the sweeps. She picks up the flags she put in earlier as we return towards the track where we started. This is what we do. All afternoon.

By four o'clock, it is nearly dark. The police search helicopter arrives and starts scouring the moor with its infrared camera. Just like we did, backwards and forwards. We're stood down for the day. The search will resume tomorrow.

When I get back home, Sally has dinner on the table. 'Giving something back,' she says and laughs. I flop down on my chair, my boots still on my feet, and let her put mashed potato and chicken casserole on my plate. She gets me a beer from the fridge and flips the cap off a second one for herself. 'No luck then?'

'No, we're continuing tomorrow morning,' I say and sigh. I make a mental note to put my walking boots to dry in front of the AGA.

'Did you know there's been a few walkers that have vanished on that route in the past?'

'Yeah, I remember the chap a few years ago. Jim told me about the other one.'

'Oh, more than two. Ronny, in the post office, told me there were well over half a dozen. In the seventies alone, they had five disappear. There was a rumour that Swaledale had its own Bermuda Triangle.'

I take a sip of my beer and let what Sally said sink in.

The next morning I put my soggy boots on, proving that I'm now too old to rely on mental notes.

'Another day, another wet moor,' Jim greets me and throws his cigarette end in a puddle.

Fewer people turn up today, as the longer the search goes on, the less interesting it becomes, unless you are the media. Then the longer he's missing, the bigger the story. This morning there are a couple of camera teams, and several journalists with their notebooks and pens ready. They move from police, to local residents, to anyone wearing a mountain rescue jacket.

'Is he likely to be alive?'

'Is the weather hampering the search?'

'Is it true that he's not the first to disappear in this location?'

Neighbouring rescue teams bring more dogs. The search area is extended and control is set up in the village of Langthwaite. A combination of 'hasty searches' and 'line searches' fills the day. To save both time and legs, farmers and gamekeepers use their quad bikes and Kawasaki mules to transport team members over rough ground to the new areas. The weather is wet and windy and by the afternoon the temperature drops sharply.

The police scale back the search late afternoon on day three. We've even combed the next section of the Coast to Coast route to no avail, just in case he overshot his original destination. Unless new evidence comes to light, such as an item of his clothing or that his credit card has been used, they'll leave his disappearance on the back burner. Inspection of the man's flat in Brighton revealed nothing to suggest that foul play has been a factor and they haven't managed to trace his family. The teams are stood down.

I throw my backpack in the back of the car and start driving home with a feeling of unease in my chest. It feels like we're letting Hans down, and the others before him. They can't all have decided to decamp to Middlesbrough. They must be out there. Somewhere.

Jim's standing outside The King's Head in Gunnerside, sucking hard on a cigarette, even though the rain is pelting down. I don't usually pop in for pints midweek, but after the previous three days, a pint with Jim is just what I need. He follows me inside.

The pub is quiet since it's a Monday. Jim has a half-drunk pint of Old Peculiar in his hand but gladly accepts another. I sit down next to him at the small wooden table in a cosy corner and stretch my legs out in front of the wood-burning stove.

'Do you know about the walkers that disappeared in the seventies? Same area.' I've been meaning to ask him since Sally told me. He pours what's left of his first pint into his mouth, leans across to put the empty glass on top of the bar and sits down again. He looks at me with one eye slightly closed.

'Who told you?' he asks.

'Sally heard it from Ronny.'

'There were rumours, but nothing more than that. It was before I joined the team.'

I take a sip of my beer. It takes effort not to gulp it down. My trousers are wet, but at least now they're warm and wet. The floor has a halfmoon-shaped damp patch marking the edge of my coat where it hangs over the back of the chair.

'Is there just one Coast to Coast route?' I ask.

'You mean across that part of the moor?'

I nod.

'Some people prefer the alternative route that goes along the valley. It's easy to get lost on the tops if the weather is bad.'

'But the day he disappeared, it was a clear day, wasn't it? The weather only turned after we started looking for him.'

'True,' Jim says and gets his packet of tobacco out. I watch him roll a cigarette, the skin on his calloused hands is full of dirt-filled cracks that look like contour lines on a map.

'Won't be long.' Jim stands up and gestures towards the door with a rollup.

To my right is an alcove with a selection of abandoned books. A couple of Dean Koontz, a Bill Bryson, and several about Swaledale's mining history. Tucked in between one of Nigella's cookbooks and an old Screwfix catalogue is a thin booklet with *Coast to Coast* written on the narrow spine. I prise it out to take a closer look. The cover is torn and shows a faded pencil drawing of a lone hiker with a large backpack. 'The

Silent Traveller's Coast to Coast' is written at the top in red in an elaborate and old-fashioned font.

I flick through the pages to find the Keld to Reeth section. The map is vague, just a few black squiggly lines, some shading to indicate valleys and hills, and a scattering of symbols marking the locations of mines and lime kilns. I'm surprised anyone managed to complete the route. I turn the page over and read the more extensive description. The route setting out from Keld sounds familiar, the bridge, the waterfalls; not much has changed in the forty years since the guide was published. It sounds idyllic and I think of that first morning with the cloud inversion.

The landlady calls in my direction. She's overheard us and is keen to get the latest gossip. I give her the bad news that he hasn't been found. She tells me about a neighbour's dog that also went missing up there ten years ago. Not found either. Her story drifts into missing sheep, cats and husbands and I lose track of who is who. I'm about to close the booklet when a particular sentence catches my eye, '*At the crossroads, continue another 100m then take a left and go through the small wooden gate…*' A small wooden gate? There?

I bring back images from the last three days, but none of them includes a small wooden gate. I flip back to the map and find the crossroads, a dashed line leaves the main track and cuts across the moorland for about a kilometre before reconnecting to the main track, cutting off a slight corner. The smell of cigarettes tells me Jim is looking over my shoulder. For a moment our eyes meet and I know we're thinking the same. I grab my damp coat from the chair, chug what's left of my pint and we leave.

'So there is more than one route across the moor,' I say to Jim. He's sitting in the passenger seat, putting new batteries into his clunky, old head torch.

'There's been slight variations over the years. Tracks appear and others get fenced off. Gamekeepers and farmers do their best to manoeuvre the walkers as far from their land as they can, even though they have no right to mess with footpaths and bridleways.'

'Did we do a line search where the guidebook mentions the gate?'

'I believe so. We did the area near the track at least. If there's still a faint path, it's worth following it and see where he might have veered off it.'

It's dark now. The rain has finally stopped and large puddles cover the road. We drive up to Surrender Bridge and turn off onto the shooting track. The tyres of my old Toyota keep slipping on the steep gravel inclines. Jim has his weatherbeaten map out and his head torch lights up a bright dot on the creased paper. I'm surprised to see a monocle in front of his right eye, held in place by his saggy skin. Genius, wish I had thought of that to save the faff of putting reading glasses on every time I need to check the map.

'Park anywhere here, we'll do the rest on foot.' Jim points to my right and I notice that we've reached the point where two shooting tracks cross each other.

We take the route signposted *C2C* while aiming our lights at the wire fence that runs parallel to the track. Occasionally it disappears from view where a fence post has rotted and fallen over. I'm starting to doubt we'll find anything when Jim's torch suddenly stops on a small, wooden gate, covered in grey lichen. It's a couple of feet wide and only the top half is visible above the heather. I'm not surprised I hadn't noticed it during the search.

Jim goes first and I follow. He's struggling to open the catch, so I look around. To the left of the gate, bits of timber are nailed horizontally to bridge it to the next fence post.

'Jim, don't bother with the catch.' I step on the lowest wooden board and swing my leg over the top of the fence. I pull my other leg over and put it down behind me on what I presume will be mossy grass.

Every muscle and every nerve ending anticipates the moment my toes will touch the ground, but the moment never comes and my leg keeps travelling downwards with my body in tow. I'm left suspended in the air, legs dangling in a hole, wiry heather brushing against my neck. My nails are digging into the wet wood of the lowest piece of timber and my other hand is grasping for bits of straggly heather.

'Fuck,' Jim shouts before he blinds me with his torch. He climbs over the fence, narrowly avoiding my fingers. As his sinewy hands get a firm hold of my wrist and he starts to pull me up, I kick with my legs, searching for something to push against. Rocks fall below me. There's another muffled scream. Jim stops pulling.

'Keep pulling, you idiot,' I shout.

'Did you hear–'

'Yes, yes. Just pull.'

Once my upper body is lying flat on the ground, I let go of the fence and push myself away from the hole. It is obscured by the heather and the soft mossy edge on the side near the gate gives no warning of the danger next to it.

'Forgot to warn you about sinkholes,' Jim mutters.

'You're fucking joking. If you honestly think–'

'Hey, you alright?' Jim is now on all fours, his light shining straight into the sinkhole.

'Am I alright? You're taking the–'

Jim hisses at me, 'Shut it, I'm not talking to you.'

I can hear a faint reply and bend down to take a look. Jim's torch is aimed at an elderly gentleman five metres or so below us. He's standing at the bottom of the hole, his arms stretched upwards, like a toddler wanting to be picked up. His lips are blue and fresh blood is trickling down his forehead.

'Thank God. Thank you so much.' His voice is shaky and he starts to cry. The sobs echo in the rocky chamber.

'We'll be right back, don't worry,' Jim reassures him, then stands up. 'Call the police, and get the team rolling.'

'What do I tell the police?'

'Tell them to bring plenty of body bags.'

It is nearly two in the morning by the time I stumble back inside the cottage. Sally is in the living room in her blue pyjamas. She puts her book down and takes off her reading glasses. The lack of a smile takes me back to the bollockings my mum used to give me.

'You could have let me know,' she says, her mouth stretched like a long hyphen across her face.

I'm about to apologise when she continues.

'I thought you were the latest victim of the Bermuda Triangle until I phoned the pub. Must have sounded like the desperate wife of an alcoholic.' She laughs and I breathe out and start taking my wet walking gear off. Soon I'm standing in my boxer shorts holding a small glass of whiskey. Sally beckons me to sit down next to her on the sofa.

'Did you find him then?'

'We did.' I don't tell her that I stepped into a sinkhole and nearly killed the missing man by showering him with rocks. I hope Jim doesn't tell anyone either. Or Hans. Maybe Hans will tell the police? A wave of anxiety travels from the pit of my stomach up to my throat. He might not even remember the rocks. By the time Jim and I had got down to help him, he was gibbering in Danish. Three days in a black hole would send anyone mad.

'Was he okay?'

This is what happens every time I attend a callout. I've explained to Sally that once we've done the job, I'm not that interested in talking about it. Especially when she asks things like: Was he injured? Did he have poor eyesight? Is he going to walk the rest of the route once he's recovered? But I know I'm not going to be allowed to go to bed unless I tell her every little detail. Or pretend I have.

She gets a whisky for herself and curls up next to me.

'So come on, tell me, were there lots of bodies down there?' she asks like I'm recounting a horror film.

'I don't know.'

'How can you not know?'

The truth is I don't want to think about it. Certainly not just before going to bed. But the thoughts come uninvited, bringing images from when team members lowered me down to help Jim strap Hans into the underground stretcher. The entrance was narrow, but the sides of the sinkhole quickly widened. The further down I went, the stronger the sour smell of death and excrement were, forcing me to breathe through my mouth. As my feet touched the bottom I heard the sound of uncooked spaghetti snapping. I'd crushed someone's rib cage. There were hints of backpacks, boots and strange deflated bundles of Gore-Tex jackets, all jumbled together in the two-metre-wide space which had been Hans' prison for the last three days. In amongst it all, the rotting carcass of a Swaledale sheep. One of its horns kept getting caught on the ropes attached to the stretcher until Jim took a firm hold, tearing the sheep's head off and tossing it aside.

I asked Jim how long he thought Hans could have survived down there.

'Longer than he would have wanted to,' he replied, in typical Jim style. He added that the first few might have died from the injuries they sustained in the fall, or from starvation. Then hydrogen sulphide and carbon dioxide from their decomposing bodies might have taken out a few more. Our misper had been lucky to have a cushion to land on and no recent casualty to foul the air. Lucky isn't exactly the word I have in mind when I think of Hans.

Sally sighs. 'You never tell me anything. Honestly, I think I'll have to join the team myself.'

'Better get your name on the waiting list then,' I reply and smile.

I'm in bed looking forward to a lie-in tomorrow morning while Sally has to get up for her shift in the charity shop. She's asleep and I'm about to drift off when images of rotting hikers appear in my mind so vividly I can smell them. For the first time in years, I've put myself in the casualty's place. My eyes flick open, I'm wide awake.

Swiftwater

The woman in the silver hatchback hesitates. Fast-flowing water is blocking the road. Still, cars overtake her, willing to take the risk.

An hour has passed since the afternoon collapsed into a thunderous cloud burst, drenching the hills, turning trickles into becks and fords into treacherous rapids. The muddy water carves an unapologetic route like it's late for an appointment with the sea.

Her legs shake as she pushes the accelerator. If she waits any longer, she'll be late picking her son up from nursery. She is halfway across when the car tilts forward and floats, the front wheels barely touching the road. She pushes hard on the accelerator just as the current spins her car sideways. The last moment her wheels make contact with the ground, the car is aimed towards the river.

A fire engine stops on a stone bridge across the bloated river. A firefighter jumps out and wrestles with his drysuit. Only minutes earlier he was enjoying a cup of tea, now it's a matter of life and death.

An older gentleman with a greyhound waves for him to look over the parapet. *There, see it?*

Four metres below, a car is stuck against the middle pillar of the bridge. The roof and most of the rear windscreen are visible above the surface, the rest submerged below the raging torrent. The firefighter needs to secure the car before a shift in the current dislodges it. Only then can he search inside it. To a river this angry, a car is just a toy that can be hurled at anything that comes in its way.

More emergency vehicles arrive from both directions and the firefighter shouts instructions to the new arrivals. *Ropes. Slings. Carabiners.* Seconds go by, but it feels like minutes. He keeps his eyes peeled on the rear windscreen. Before the ropes are in place the only thing he can do is call out to the casualty or aim his throwline at them and hope they're strong enough to hold on. But he can't see anyone inside. No one has their face crammed into the air pocket remaining in the tiny roof space, no one is pushing at the doors trying to get out. He scans the banks of the river and the base of the bridge hoping to see someone clinging to a branch or a rock.

His colleagues use a rope to lower him towards the brown water rushing beneath his feet. He pulls the deformed doors to create a gap large enough to fasten a sling around the pillar. A minute later the car is secured by two ropes. Now he has time to look inside while the water tugs at him, keen to drag him downstream.

The husband pulls up on the drive to the modern four-bed house he moved into six months ago. On his doorstep is a female police officer, peering into the glazed section of the front door. He curses and assumes there's been another burglary on the estate. She turns, spots him and lowers her head. His fury fades into fear.

Madeleine Prusser, she says. She keeps talking but her words don't reach his brain.

The man holds on to the car door and looks at his feet for a few seconds. *Joshua?*

He struggles to unlock his phone, his hands shaking too much. He phones his wife. There's no answer. He scrolls back and forth until he locates the number for his son's nursery.

Twenty minutes later, he's cradling his son tightly in his arms. A nursery nurse tries to reassure him. *They'll find her, don't worry. Her phone probably got wet, that's why it's going straight to voicemail.*

What was she wearing? the husband is asked half an hour later by a man wearing a mountain rescue jacket. He can't remember. *White jumper, black trousers maybe? She has a green jacket. But she loves the grey one. It's warmer.* The harder he thinks, the more uncertain he becomes. The stress makes his voice wobble. *I don't know,* he says, resting his forehead in his hands.

The police have taken him to a farmyard from where the mountain rescue tem is coordinating the search. A steady stream of people arrive donning dry suits, buoyancy aids and helmets. Five rescuers carry a large inflatable boat towards the fast-flowing river at the bottom of one of the fields, while others are given instructions to comb the banks on either side.

People reassure him they are doing everything they can but won't say that things will be alright. He's handed a lukewarm cup of tea by a community support officer. Radio messages drift out of the mountain rescue van in a steady stream. A lot of people are out searching.

Does she have a turquoise waterproof? asks a rescuer, leaning out of the van.

He shakes his head, but a moment later his stomach sinks. *Yes, sorry. She does. And she's wearing a dark blue Fair Isle sweater.* He remembers now. That morning, Joshua spilt his cereal across the kitchen table. The milk soaked the sleeve of Madeleine's white cardigan and she changed into the jumper he'd given her for Christmas.

They'll bring it over for you to identify.

Ten minutes later, a woman in a drysuit walks across the farmyard with his wife's raincoat in her hand. She's intercepted by another team member who hands her a pair of trousers and something small and pink. His heart sinks.

He nods at the jacket. *Yes, that's hers.* He holds up the trousers but hands them back straight away. They are far too big to be Madeleine's. He sees the pink bra but doesn't understand. *Have you found her?* He gets no response and looks around for someone who might tell him. People disperse as they are given new instructions. He runs back to the van and puts his head inside. *Has she been found!?*

A startled team member shakes his head. *Sorry, no.* He returns to the laptop to capture the information that trickles in via the radios.

The sun sets and one by one vehicles leave. The police drop the husband off at his mother's house where Joshua is waiting. He doesn't know what to tell his son when he asks where Mummy has gone.

A text message from the police wakes the mountain rescue team's swiftwater lead at 7 am after a fitful night's sleep. Since the previous evening, his thoughts have been dominated by death and bloated corpses. Finding Madeleine's clothes had been bad news. The river can strip a person of their clothing, but only if they are unconscious or dead.

He kisses his wife's hair, slides out of bed and heads for the bathroom. He passes the message onto the team, letting them know that a police search dog has picked up a scent at a weir six miles downstream. He's relieved that his stomach survived the river water he swallowed the day before. From the replies, it turns out not everyone has been so lucky.

Dogwalkers and early-rising toddlers with bleary-eyed parents have claimed the river paths. It's Saturday and the sun is shining. For most, the previous day's storm is already a faint memory. Birds repair their nests along the banks and morning dew still covers the playground equipment.

The arrival of police and mountain rescue vehicles attracts a crowd. People are pointing to something downstream of the weir. It appears and then disappears, trapped in a treacherous stopper, where hydraulic forces will forever circulate objects until either they sink or the flow changes. Swimmers, kayakers, paddle boarders, as well as rescue technicians, have met their demise in a seemingly harmless stopper.

The rescue lead is concerned. The most experienced technicians are either on holiday or at home vomiting their guts out. The ones that have turned up have only recently qualified and it's their first real rescue. Some have never even seen a dead body. They stare at him wide-eyed as he explains how they're going to recover what is trapped in the water.

His team is nervous. They're making mistakes, getting the ropes tangled and barking orders at each other. People are watching. The lead gathers everyone to correct the ropework, to ask for more air to be added to the inflatable boat and to make sure everyone has understood exactly what is expected of them. Thankfully, there's no rush, not anymore.

The boat is secured from all sides by ropes to prevent it from getting trapped in the stopper or washed away by the flow. Five technicians, including the rescue lead, wade out into knee-deep water and climb inside. They feel the power of the water while they are dragged into position close to where the object has been spotted. So far everything is working well. It's just like they've practised. They wait like this for a couple of minutes, until someone sees something white two metres river-left of the dinghy. The ropes are adjusted and the rescue lead leans over the bow and reaches into the water. It's just a plastic bag.

River-right! There! See it?

This time there is no doubt as to what's trapped below the weir. They are close enough to spot a glimpse of blond hair as it's sucked below the surface. The lead calls the police on his radio handset. *Casualty located. Will begin the recovery.* The officers begin to clear the bank of onlookers, some of whom are filming on mobile phones. They reluctantly move further down the path while still hoping to catch sight of the corpse.

Four strong arms get hold of a naked leg and they pull as hard as they can. The water is reluctant to surrender its catch, but they manage to drag the cold and battered body into the boat. The left knee is fractured making the lower leg point at an impossible angle. The lead leans across the side of the boat and vomits. Maybe he wasn't so lucky after all.

An hour later, it's like it's never happened. A few joggers and young children on pushbikes pass the weir, unaware of the drama that played out that morning. Not so on the internet where videos of the naked corpse are shared and liked. Comments are either crude or lecturing. A few miles downstream a blue Fair Isle jumper is stuck on a branch hanging into the water. Eight months later, it is still there, covered in green algae.

Five years later, the video makes another round around social media. That night the husband drinks a whole bottle of whisky to suppress the images that play over and over again inside his brain. He prays that Josua will never see it, but knows he probably will.

The memory will remain with the rescuers forever and haunt them for weeks. Some describe what they saw to their partners, over and over again, while others won't tell anyone. The more experienced team members reassure them that next time it'll be easier. They all know there will always be a next time.

Who's a Good Doggie?

When I enter the kitchen two glasses of red wine are already on the table. I'm shaking with frustration while pools of water form on the flagged-stone floor below my rain-soaked coat. My husband Gavin is frying onions on the solid-fuel AGA.

'Has she done another runner?' he asks.

I nod. I'm not sure how much sarcasm is in his voice, but I can guess what's coming next.

'Maybe you should keep her on the lead then?'

I draw a deep breath. Stay calm. Nope. I shout, 'She's a fucking search dog. She's not supposed to be on a bloomin' lead. And why the fuck did you name her Fifi!' I stomp out of the kitchen. Owning a search dog shouldn't mean you have a dog you constantly have to go and search for, but that's how it feels.

I remember picking Fifi up from a local farm when she was eight weeks old. She stood out from a litter of six with her alert blue eyes and dainty white-tipped tail waving proudly in the air. Apart from her white socks, the rest of her body was glossy black. A perfect collie. She excelled in the puppy classes, relishing every challenge and picking up new commands faster than any other dog I'd had before.

Fifi was eight months old when our local mountain rescue team announced a search-dog taster session in the local park. A pick-and-mix of dog breeds, ranging from a chihuahua in a pink jumper to a huge Doberman, all eyeing each other up on arrival. Apart from Fifi, there was only one other collie. I exchanged smug glances with its owner. We both knew what a search dog should look like.

While a boxer was humping the instructor's leg and two Jack Russells were scrapping in a corner, Fifi sat perfectly still and listened. To test their searching instinct we had to hide their toys and then set them off to find them. Fifi needed only ten seconds to locate her purple dinosaur behind a bush and drop him at the feet of the instructor. Three months later, Fifi, Gavin and I joined the rescue team and started our training. That was two years ago.

Gavin sets the table while my nose is pressed against the kitchen window. We live in a remote cottage, surrounded by fields divided by ancient stone walls. The sheep were brought down to the valley bottoms for lambing a week ago and the ground-nesting curlews and lapwings haven't yet arrived back from their winter hangouts. As long as Fifi comes back, there's little harm in letting her romp around for a bit. That's what my brain tells me, but my heart struggles to agree. Minutes pass and my worry grows. I take a sip of wine.

'Maybe I should look into those GPS tracking devices?' I suggest to Gavin.

'You need a mobile signal for those.' He pricks a potato in the pot of boiling water to check if it's soft.

The way he just keeps cooking annoys me. Like the food is more important than our dog. If Fifi doesn't get back soon, dinner will be spoiled anyway. I return to the window. It's getting dark and the rain is still pelting down. I finish the wine and think about having a refill when there's a faint scratch on the front door. There she is, thin and wet, with excited eyes staring up at me. She trots in and shakes her fur to paint little brown marks across the hallway walls.

'Thank God you're back!' I grab a towel from the basket next to the shoe rack and rub the worst of the rain and mud off Fifi's coat.

'Great timing, dinner's ready,' Gavin announces from the kitchen.

We sit down to lamb stew and potatoes served with last year's wild garlic that had been resurrected from the freezer. After a couple of mouthfuls, both mine and Gavin's phones bleep. A callout. Missing climber. Male, 35 years old. Oxnop Scar area.

'Great timing,' I reply and sigh. You never know how long a search might go on for so I start shoving burning hot stew into my mouth. I also need something to soak up the red wine.

'At least it's local,' Gavin says and covers his plate with foil.

I put Fifi in her fluorescent orange vest that has a bell and a flashing red light stuck to its back. On the sides, it says 'SEARCH DOG' in large reflective letters. If the text message and our reaction haven't been enough of a hint, then getting the vest out is proof that it's time to work. She looks shattered.

'I bet you wish you hadn't gone off and done all that running about now,' I say and start putting my soaking wet waterproofs back on.

We set off, hoping it won't take long to locate the missing man.

*

'Well done Fifi! What a good girl.' I ruffle the fur behind her ears and she licks my face with her agile pink tongue. 'Wasn't she amazing, finding the body so quickly?'

Gavin and I are curled up on the sofa watching TV with Fifi between us. Gavin gives her a stroke and is also rewarded with a brief facewash.

'Their noses are truly amazing. You'd have thought the rain would make it almost impossible. Shame we were too late,' I say with a sigh.

'Yeah, but I bet the chap died on impact.'

It's nearly eleven and we've only just finished dinner. Even though it only took Fifi ten minutes to find him, we then had to wait for a senior police officer to drive from Durham to come and rule out foul play. The scene was typical enough: a climber at the base of a cliff with the rope on top of him, but of course they needed to do things by the book. The man's face was unrecognisable, and his limbs were in disarray, but what I can't forget is his right hand, or rather what was left of it. All the fingers gone and half the palm replaced by bits of stringy meat, vivid red in the torchlight.

'Wasn't that a bit weird? The man's hand–'

'Probably a fox,' Gavin interrupts. 'Will mention it to Barry on Friday. Gamekeepers don't want foxes around here.'

A week goes by. Fifi runs off a few times, but returns before we become too worried. She always seems to know her way back. We visit friends in Stalling Busk for Sunday lunch and work off the Yorkshire puddings with a brisk walk up to Stake Moss. One second Fifi is running along the path, nose to the ground, the next, she is nowhere to be seen. The fog drops on us like a damp woollen hat, quenching our shouts to attract her attention. For every minute that passes, the adrenaline levels increase in my bloodstream. We are far away from home. She doesn't know this area.

'Let's go back down. She might have returned to the village,' Gavin suggests.

I call for Fifi at regular intervals while we make our way down the hill, even though her name embarrasses me. And there she is, sitting by the front door of our friends' house, wagging her tail. We thank them for a lovely day and head home ready to put our feet up and watch 'All Creatures Great and Small'.

I am soaking in the bath when the message comes through. Missing walker above Stalling Busk. 72 year old female. Blue jacket, green backpack.

'Oh for fuck's sake. Couldn't they have reported her missing while we were there!' I try my hardest to put on walking trousers without falling over. My thighs are damp and hot, offering too much friction to easily slip into each leg.

We get back to Stalling Busk as light fades. A police vehicle is already on the scene and our friends are talking to an officer explaining that we'd been up on the moor that afternoon but not seen anyone. A team vehicle arrives and our search manager gives me the nod to take Fifi to do some air scenting before the hillside becomes littered with humans all oozing enticing odours.

Fifi sets off and I follow. To my annoyance, she stays close as we work our way up the hillside. 'Come on girl, do your thing! Don't hang around me.' I wave for her to run wide to scan large areas for the smell of humans, but she refuses to leave my side. The fog has lifted somewhat and I start to think I have a better chance of spotting the missing lady than Fifi has.

She comes to an abrupt halt.

'What?' I ask. We are almost at the spot where I'd lost sight of her earlier that day.

Fifi gives me a peculiar look before she turns towards the stone wall and jumps straight over it.

'You'd better not!' I shout at her, worried she'd decided to run off instead of continuing to search. I peer over the wall to not lose sight of her and see her tracking a straight path at high-speed disappearing beyond a brow. I can't tell if she is scenting or just running off. To my relief, she returns a few seconds later, barking to let me know she's found something. I clamber over the wall, having made sure there isn't a disapproving farmer lurking nearby, and let her guide me across the grassy moor.

A slim body, dressed in blue, is lying face down on the ground. Oh Lord, another dead one. I reward Fifi by giving her the purple dinosaur. It's been patched beyond recognition but it's still her favourite. I turn the lady over, look for breathing and try to locate a pulse. Nothing. I radio control with the exact location. They'll send medical assistance. I'm about to start CPR when I spot that there's blood on the woman's sleeve. Her fingers have been gnawed off. Another fox? Fifi watches my every move as I start doing chest compressions.

Winter turns into spring and the number of callouts increases considerably. We have an unusually high incidence of walkers who suffer fatal slips from crags, and one man bleeds to death from unexplained cuts to the arteries in his ankle. The area gets a reputation for being more dangerous than it looks and begins to attract people who otherwise would have aimed for more exciting regions in Scotland or the Lakes. The media finds out about the foxes that keep mutilating the casualties and the gamekeepers assure the journalist that they are dealing with it. Tourism blossoms. Everyone is happy. My pride grows as Fifi proves herself again and again.

'Do you think Fifi has taught herself to smell dead people?' I ask Gavin one day.

'Possibly. I suppose none of the other search dogs have as much experience with smells from corpses since we always practise with live volunteers.'

I briefly wonder if, out of fairness, we ought to try to find a dead person to help us train but dismiss the idea as too complicated. My attention returns to the framed certificate that shows that Fifi has been the most successful search dog in the country during the month of May. I hang it on the wall in the living room, next to the ones she was rewarded for March and April.

'You're a good doggie, aren't you!' She looks as proud as Gavin and I do as we stand back to admire the collection of awards.

'Oh, I nearly forgot, here's another one,' Gavin says and fishes out a thin gold ring from his trouser pocket. He holds it up between his thumb and finger and smiles. They keep appearing at the bottom of the garden, where Fifi does her toileting last thing at night. He pops it into the cut glass bowl on the sideboard with the others.

'Watch, she's doing that thing again,' I say and point to Fifi who has started to pace back and forth looking at the hill packs that we have ready by the front door. 'You know, I think she can sense another callout, don't you?' A minute later our phones go off. *'Unresponsive male mountain biker with severe injuries. Found on Fremington Edge.'*

'Back to Fremington Edge then!' I announce. 'You really are a good doggie, Fifi.'

A Cross on Your Foot

A young woman in a blue fleece jacket stands in the middle of the hamlet of quaint stone cottages. Her red hair is tied into a ponytail and her hands are tucked under her arms.

Esme Wintrip? Sam calls out. She runs up to his car, her tense face expectant with hope.

Mountain Rescue? she asks.

Sam nods.

He has never been the first to arrive at a callout before. His red mountain rescue jacket and the background radio traffic make him more confident, but still, he feels like he's playing a role, imitating what he's heard others say, pretending he's up to the task because the woman in front of him thinks he is.

My dad's up there, on the fell. I think he's broken his foot. This matches the information passed to the rescue team by the ambulance crew who won't arrive for another forty minutes. She keeps talking, describing their route, saying they've come up from Shropshire, she's a florist and her father is a retired dentist. Sam nods while trying to keep up with the information passed over the team radios, too polite to ask her to be quiet.

Only ten minutes ago, Sam was writing an email to his new boss, listing the projects he's contributing to. Things are getting back to normal, whatever that means. Everyone is returning to the office. No more working from home. Every new memo seemed determined to take away the life he'd got used to. Soon he would have to leave the Dales and move back to Birmingham.

He picks up his radio handset and draws a deep breath. Esme falls quiet.

Rescue-Control from Rescue-Sam.

Rescue-Sam, this is Rescue-Control, pass your message.

With Esme Wintrip, the informant. The casualty is her father, Brendon Wintrip. Will get back to you with more info shortly.

From the vague directions Esme gives him, the casualty could be more than three kilometres away. Sam scans the map but finds no roads that might shorten the route. What seemed like a quick, uncomplicated callout might take hours longer than he anticipated. He checks his watch, worried he won't make it back for the meeting with his new boss.

A farmer pulls up next to them on a quad bike. Sam shows him the spot on the map where he thinks the casualty might be.

Aye, aye… Through those fields, through the gates, brings you 'round t'corner of that hill. Rough track for half mile or so. Won't make it in that. The farmer points to Sam's small Toyota hatchback.

Sam is torn between letting Esme take him up the same route she came down, which would guarantee finding her father, or taking this other route most likely to be used by the team vehicles for evacuating the casualty. Esme stares at him, wanting him to take charge. Sam's confidence fades. He wishes the rest of the team would arrive soon. Why on earth did he think arriving first was something to aim for?

The tension is broken when Dave arrives in a 4X4.

Simple, Dave says after being briefed. *I drive up this way and you follow Esme.*

Esme takes Sam along a steep and rocky path at a furious pace. The colours of the hills are dulled by the weak January light. The bracken has turned brown and icicles cling to the side of the stream next to the path. The cold air is squeezing his chest as he breathes heavily to keep up. But even at this rate, he will be late for his meeting, with no means of letting anyone know.

Half an hour later, they emerge from the gully onto an exposed hillside. The wind bites at his ears. Sam worries about how cold her father must be, not having been able to move for nearly two hours. He pulls a black beanie from his pocket and offers it to Esme. She shakes her head, not even slowing down. He asks her if it's much further but instead of answering she speeds up. He soon spots four people, walkers by the looks of it, gathered around a figure sitting on the ground.

Esme's father has a pink hat on his head and a purple fleece wrapped across his shoulders. Someone has draped a blue waterproof jacket over his legs. His left foot points in the wrong direction, like it's no longer part of his body. Sam tries not to grimace. The man is pale and struggles to speak when Sam asks him for his name and age.

Brendon Wintrip, 62.

Dad, Esme interrupts, *you're 63. Your birthday was last week.*

Did you fall? Sam asks.

No, he didn't. Just put his foot on a wobbly rock.

While Brendon isn't keen to speak, the walkers who have stopped to help are falling over themselves to tell Sam everything they have done. A tall woman in an expensive down jacket keeps offering help, making it difficult for him to measure Brendon's breathing and pulse. He hopes none of them notices his hands shaking. It's the first time he's examining a real casualty, but he can't tell them that.

Sam looks at the man's twisted foot. It's dislocated or broken, or maybe both. Probably won't kill him, but hypothermia might, given the time it will take to get him off this hillside.

On a scale from 1 to 10, how painful is your ankle?

Nine, the man answers in a weak voice, head bent down and eyes closed.

He tries to judge how cold Brendon is, but it is hard to tell what is a reaction to the pain and what is due to decreasing levels of consciousness. He's only barely able to stay upright.

Sam takes a foam pad out of his backpack. *Here, sit on this.* With Esme's help, he slides the pad underneath Brendon, insulating him from the cold ground and buying a bit more time.

He calls control with a list of kit: *the large medical pack, stretcher, casualty bag, and splint bag. And make sure we get the defib, just in case. No cardiac symptoms, but he's hypothermic, not sure how severe yet.* As he says the words, it suddenly hits him. If he doesn't handle this right he might kill this man. The cold blood from Brendon's legs could flood his heart and he could suffer a cardiac arrest. Before Sam joined the team, he had no idea this could happen.

He's relieved to see Dave approach on foot up the hill from a different direction.

Sorry, took a wrong turn. I've marked the correct route for the team vehicles.

Sam cranes his neck and spots Dave's car halfway up the hill.

Happy for me to take over the cas care? he asks.

Sam nods in relief. Dave's a trainee paramedic.

Hi Brendon, my name's Dave. I'm going to get you warmed up and a bit more comfortable before we take you off the hill, okay?

Dave unfolds an orange group shelter and waves for Esme to join him and Brendon inside. Sam stands on the edge of the shelter to stop the breeze from sneaking through. He listens to the matter-of-fact way Dave talks to the casualty. *I'm going to remove your boot to check the blood flow to your foot, alright? It's going to hurt.*

The man moans. No one says anything. Sam worries that something has gone wrong when Dave speaks.

I've drawn a cross on the top of your foot where I can feel your pulse so I don't have to look for it again. What's your pain score? Nine, did you say? I've got some paracetamol I can give you. We've got stronger stuff coming.

Other team members arrive carrying equipment. They are red-faced from the effort. Splints are fed into the tent as well as a cylinder of laughing gas for pain relief. But no laughs are coming from the tent, only the occasional groan.

The team carries Brendon down the hill, with three volunteers on each side of the stretcher. Wrapped up in a thermal silver blanket inside a casualty bag, he's warm and the pain from his ankle seems manageable.

He chats happily to the people around him and apologises for being an inconvenience.

Nothing to apologise for, Sam says. *Just bad luck. You didn't plan to break your foot.*

If I had, the man answers, *I would have picked a spot closer to the road.* He laughs and winces in pain. *I'm sure you have better things to do than traipsing up and down this hill.*

Sam stops smiling and checks the time. There's no way he'll be back in time for his meeting. He tries to come up with a plausible excuse. What could be better than saving someone's life? But he knows it's not good enough. There is nothing humane about their human resources department. No exceptions. They made that clear. Being late for the meeting just proves how he can't be trusted to work from home any more.

Will he be okay? Esme asks Sam when they're getting close to the team vehicle.

I think so, he replies.

I can't thank you enough for everything you've done. You're all amazing, she says.

Sam is proud, but mostly relieved, that everything has gone well so far. Would this be the last time he felt like this? Soon he might have to hand his radio and jacket back. For what? A life commuting and sitting behind a desk in a room full of unhappy people?

You're so lucky. I'd do anything to live in the Dales. It's so beautiful, and everyone seems to know everyone else, Esme continues.

He doesn't mention that it might be coming to an end sooner than he'd wished. Instead, he stays silent, placing each foot in front of the other staring at the ground. A fuzzy feeling spreads through his body. He doesn't know why until he hears himself speak.

Yes, same here. I'd do anything to stay. It's obvious now. He'll check with people in the team, in the pub, in the post office. Everyone knows everyone else. Someone will give him a job. Maybe he'll retrain, it's not the end of the world.

When they reach the team's Land Rover, the rear seats have been removed to accommodate the stretcher. They drive Brendon to the village where he's handed into the experienced hands of the ambulance crew. The other team members head off in the direction they came, keen to pick up their day where they left off.

Sam sets off in a desperate dash to get home for his meeting. He's twenty minutes late when he logs on to his video call on his laptop. Only then he spots the dark smear of mud that covers his left cheek. His boss looks up from her keyboard and tilts her head with a puzzled look. She's about to say something when Sam intervenes. *Sorry, I'm late, but there's something I need to tell you.*

What Kind of Mountain Rescuer Are You?

1. You are woken by a message at 1 am. A young man has gone missing from the Tan Hill Inn, the highest and most isolated pub in Britain. What do you do?

    A. Go back to sleep pretending you left your phone downstairs and didn't hear the message. (Go to 2)

    B. Get dressed as slowly as you can hoping he might be found before you set off. (Go to 3)

    C. Dash out of bed and jump into your car hoping you find him quickly so you can go back to bed. (Go to 4)

2. You wake up at 7 am to the headlines that Ed Sheeran got lost in thick fog between the pub and his luxury campervan and gave everyone who helped search for him a ticket and airfare to his next concert in Barbados. You vow to never ignore a callout ever again. (Go to 1)

3. An hour later you arrive at Tan Hill Inn to discover that you are the first on scene. What do you do?

A. Go inside and have a pint as the pub is still serving and you deserve it after the sacrifices you've made. (Go to 5)
B. Decide to control the search since you too have a habit of getting lost on the way home from the pub and feel you can tap into the psychological profile of the missing person. (Go to 6)
C. Wait in your car until a more experienced team member arrives and then pretend you had just arrived. (Go to 9)

4. Only when you are stopped by the police and breathalyzed, do you remember the bottle of wine you drank with your spaghetti bolognese earlier in the evening. You vow never to drink and drive again. (Go to 1)

5. You forget about the callout and start a conversation with a sociable fellow at the bar. Two pints later you realise that the man is the missing person. What do you do?

A. Quickly accept his offer to stay in his campervan. In the morning, you sneak off and make an anonymous phone call to the police saying they should search his van again. (Go to 15)

B. Ask him to pretend that you found him in a ditch around the corner and present him to control so everyone can go home. (Go to 16)
C. Inform control that you happened to befriend the missing man on your arrival two hours earlier but hadn't realised until now who he was. (Go to 17)

6. You approach the attending police officer who says he has already searched the pub and the area close to it, as well as checked all the campervans parked nearby. What do you do?

A. Having trust issues, you dispatch the first couple of team members to search both inside and outside the pub again. You tell them to thoroughly search all the campervans again in case someone is hiding the missing man. (Go to 7)
B. Return to your car and draw up search areas on your battered OS map. (Go to 8)
C. Accept that your experience of missing person behaviour doesn't include anyone lost on the moor in inclement weather and you hand over responsibility to the team's search management leader as soon as she arrives on the scene. (Go to 9)

7. Your team members return triumphantly, dragging the missing man between them. They found him at the bar too drunk to remember his name and too wobbly-legged to return to his campervan. (Go to 17)

8. You follow all the rules about conducting a search operation for a missing person and make the team crisscross the wet moor for hours without a break. Team members are tired, hungry and irritable. What do you do?

   A. Tell everyone to go and enjoy coffee and sausage sandwiches provided free by the pub in gratitude for their efforts. (Go to 7)
   B. Tell them a man's life is dependent on them and give them new areas to search. (Go to 10)

9. The search coordinator asks for a volunteer to check that the missing person isn't inside the pub. What do you do?

   A. Decide searching indoors is beneath your sophisticated training and supreme fitness; it's a job for someone feeble and inexperienced, not for you. (Go to 11)
   B. Jump at the opportunity - as not only could you sneak in a cheeky pint but it would also be warm and dry. (Go to 12)

10. At 10 am everyone is on their eighth hour of searching. You, on the other hand, are dry and comfortable but in need of emptying your bladder. You nip to the pub toilets hoping nobody calls you on the radio. While sitting on the toilet you see an arm sticking out from the adjacent cubicle. On closer inspection, it turns out to be the missing man who has died from choking on his vomit. What do you do next?

- A. Blame the team for not having checked that the missing person wasn't in the pub. (Go to 15)
- B. Apologise to the team and blame it on the police officer who told you they had already checked the pub. (Go to 16)

11. You volunteer for the most remote and treacherous area and sigh loudly when you are assigned some newly qualified team members to join your search party. What do you do?

- A. Take the opportunity to pass on your wealth of experience to the group by telling them about every time you would have found the missing person if it hadn't been for the poor search management by control. (Go to 13)
- B. Ask your group condescendingly whether anyone needs the toilet before you head off, and

roll your eyes when one of them says yes. (Go to 14)

12. Since you are inside the pub, you take the opportunity to visit the toilets and notice an arm sticking out from the adjacent cubicle. It's the missing man and he's making some unpleasant gurgling noises. You realise that he's choking on his vomit and shoulder-barge the door to get inside. You clear his airways, getting your hands covered in his sick, before putting him in the recovery position. You've saved his life. (Go to 15)

13. At 10 am you get a call to return to control. Your search group are far behind since they lack your supreme fitness and keep stopping for snacks. When they finally catch up with you, it turns out one of your team members has gone missing and you spend the next two hours searching for him, too embarrassed to let control know. (Go to 15)

14. The new team member runs out of the pub shouting that someone is dying in the men's toilets. You run inside and manage to stop the man from choking on his vomit. The man turns out to be the missing person and you take credit for both finding him and saving his life. (Go to 16)

15. You suffer from too much pride and don't have enough compassion for your fellow team members. Since the mountain rescue team is a charity, unless you do something really stupid, your team members have to suffer your presence until you decide to retire.

16. You are good at covering up your flaws while preventing anyone from suffering unnecessarily. You always wear your red jacket even when grocery shopping to make your neighbours believe you are a superhero. Your fellow team members aren't convinced.

17. You are an outstanding asset to the team. Your intuition and experience are second to none and it is doubtful the team could operate without you. Congratulations!

Ruby

Ruby! The old man's voice is lost in the misty moorland air. *Ruuuby! Come here!* He supports himself on a walking stick while shuffling back and forth along the rough farm track. His eyes search the waist-high bracken towards the crest of the hill where the coarse grass gives way to purple heather, the pasture turning into moorland. A minute ago, the russet cocker spaniel was chasing rabbits through the dense vegetation. Now, she's nowhere to be seen. *Ruuuby!*

His phone rings.

Dad! It's me. How's it going?

He doesn't get a chance to reply as his daughter barks something at his two grandsons in the background.

Sorry! We're going out for dinner, just trying to get the boys ready.

They're in Portugal, a last-minute booking because it's rained all August. Next week the boys will be back at school.

I hope Ruby and Flipper are behaving, she said as if she's apologising for the inconvenience she has caused.

The old man looks down at Flipper sitting patiently by his feet. He's a wobbly black spaniel with grey streaks around his muzzle and poor eyesight. He doesn't stray far, not like Ruby. *Yes, yes. They're fine.*

Great. Got to go. The boys are still wearing their swimming trunks!

He presses the screen a few times before he manages to disconnect the call. Flipper looks at him with worried eyes.

The man knows this track from years ago when he worked in the nearby quarry. It wasn't so muddy then.

Dark clouds approach from the west and it starts to rain. First just a few fat drops here and there, then more persistently. His hip aches and his throat is raw from shouting. He looks at his watch - an hour has passed. The light fades as he makes his way towards his car, turning his head several times hoping to see her bounding down the hill. The only animals present are some Swaledale sheep grazing calmly, and they pay him no attention.

Waiting in his Toyota with the wipers squeaking across the windscreen, he can just make out the end of the track where he hopes Ruby will appear. Flipper curls up and falls asleep on the passenger seat and soon the car smells of wet dog. The old man doesn't want to leave. What if she turns up? What is he going to say to his daughter? He gives Flipper a stroke. The spaniel lifts an eyelid before going back to sleep.

The man is on the brink of dozing off when bright headlights make him shield his eyes with the back of his hand. A gamekeeper dressed in dark green waterproofs approaches his car with a shotgun case slung across his shoulder.

How do? Waiting for someone?

He tells the gamekeeper about his missing dog.

I'll look out for her. The gamekeeper drives up the track in his Japanese 4x4. The roar of the engine fades away and darkness settles once more.

The old man turns his sidelights on and reclines his seat to get comfortable. He rests his eyes on the track but soon falls asleep. An hour later, he wakes in a panic, convinced he has heard a shot. Flipper is still asleep. It must have been a dream.

He wakes again at two in the morning, stiff from sleeping upright. The rain has stopped, and the air is cold. The full moon throws a shimmer over the valley, showing off the faint brows of the hills against the ink-blue sky. He circles the car and peers down the track. *Ruuuuby!* He walks up to the stonewall and unzips his trousers, his eyes turned towards the sky. Before pulling his zip up, he remembers reading somewhere that dogs can recognise the smell of their owner's wee. He shakes a few drops onto the track, just in case.

He returns to the car. In a few hours, it will be light enough to resume the search.

A knock on the window makes Flipper bark. It's dawn. A round-faced farmer with gappy teeth breathes condensation on the window. *Missing dog, aye. Did you check 'em holes?*

The old man doesn't know of any holes.

It's a limestone pavement, like. Full of sinkholes. Lost many a ewe down 'em over t'years. I'll show you.

The farmer drives his quad bike down the uneven track with a collie perched behind him like its paws have been nailed down. The old man follows.

The farmer stops the quad bike by the bracken and looks at the gentleman. His back is bent and his steps tentative as he struggles along the path. Poor chap. He feels the man's pain. He switches the engine off and wades into the dense ground cover, gesturing to his dog to remain by the bike. The morning dew wets his jeans and the sleeves of his fleece jacket.

There's a hole somewhere 'round here, he calls out. A few seconds later, he spots it. The grassy edges droop downwards to reveal a dark opening a couple of feet across. He bends down and listens. Nothing. *Can't hear her, but that doesn't mean she's not down there.* Mountain rescue pulled out one of his ewes from a similar hole last year. Her bleats had drawn the attention of some walkers. This is different.

The farmer looks at the old man, who's smiling even though worry lines are still present across his forehead. It's the look of a man whose hope has been reignited. That swings it. He gets his phone out, dials 999 and asks for the police, followed by mountain rescue. The last thing he needs is an old chap trying to go down the hole himself.

The farmer returns to his quad bike and reassures the man that help is on the way.

How deep is it? The old man asks.

Deep like, twenty, thirty foot maybe.

The old man shakes his head and looks down at his feet. Surely no dog could survive such a fall. He's told not to leave until rescue arrives. The farmer drives off. The collie keeps his accusing eyes fixed on him from its position on the back of the bike. *Thank you*, he shouts, but the farmer can't hear him over the sound of the engine.

The old man wants to take a closer look at the hole, but fears he might stumble on the rough ground. Or even worse, fall into it. So he stands still and waits. The chill of the morning air makes him shiver. He's tempted to drop onto his haunches but isn't sure he'd be able to get up again. Wisps of low mist rise from the bottom of the valley, joining the grey clouds. It's six thirty. Christ, he's such a tosser. The rescue team isn't going to thank him for getting them out of bed at such an early hour when it's not even certain Ruby is down there. His heart jumps around inside his chest, fuelled by worry.

Forty minutes later, a red Nissan Jimny crawls up the track. A mountain rescue Land Rover is not far behind, followed by a grey pickup. He waits, frozen to the ground in his grey jacket and blue corduroy trousers. People in mountain rescue jackets pour out of the first two vehicles. One man has pillow creases still visible across his face. A television crew emerges from the pickup; a young girl in a pink hoodie and ripped jeans, a lanky lad with a thick ginger beard and a lardy bloke in a grey sweatshirt carrying a heavy film camera. 'Avocado-on-toast' people, he would have called them if they had turned up on his street in Darlington.

The old man points to the spot where the farmer said the hole was. A few minutes later the rescue is in full swing. He gives permission for the crew to film. If it helps the team's fundraising, how could he possibly refuse? The fat lad sticks his camera in his face but their questions are stupid. *Do you feel grateful for the people coming to the rescue? What went through your mind when you realised Ruby might be in the hole? Any advice to give dog walkers that come to the area?* He finds himself snarling at the girl and the TV crew soon drifts towards the hole where the action is.

A safe route to the sinkhole is marked with flags since it turns out there are several holes hidden in the vegetation. A couple of people get changed into caving suits and helmets, while others carry bags of rope and wire ladders. Stakes are hammered into the ground to provide anchor points. More rescuers arrive on foot and soon the bracken is home to an army of people in red jackets calling instructions to each other, with the television crew darting back and forth. All the old man can do is watch and hope. He doesn't want Ruby to be found in the hole, but if she's down there, finding her body will at least give some closure.

A rescuer approaches him, eyebrows lowered, throwing the occasional glance behind him for support from his team. *We haven't found her, sorry.*

The old man is unsure how to respond and in the end just nods.

We'll check the other sinkholes while we're here.

The team moves a few metres to the right. The ropes are long enough, so only a few minutes go by until someone announces that Ruby isn't in the second hole either. This is repeated a couple of times. The lad with the ginger beard feels the cold and returns to their pickup. Rather than moving around to capture close-ups of team members entering and emerging from sinkholes, the cameraman stands still and does a few panoramic shots across the valley.

The old man feels guilty for causing such upheaval, especially since Ruby doesn't seem to be present, dead or alive. Maybe they are waiting for him to give them permission to stop searching. That's when the team gathers in a spot to the left of the original hole.

She's the newest member and everyone is staring at her, especially at her chest. They are assessing her size.

I think she'll fit, someone says. They gather around a tiny opening in the ground while a couple of people tear at the turf to get a better view of what's beneath. It's a narrow hole and the limestone sides make it difficult to widen any further.

She'll have to take her helmet off, someone adds. She doesn't mind. It always makes her head look like an orange mushroom.

And your bra. You need to be able to let your breasts move around freely, a female team member whispers.

The new team member is handed a caving suit. She hides behind the team vehicle and gets undressed down to her knickers. The wind bites into her exposed skin and the suit feels damp and rough. She returns to the group who are pleased that they're able to tighten her harness even more now the extra layers of clothing have been removed. She feels small, smaller than she's ever felt before. *It's just the opening that's tight, it will widen once you're inside.*

She has to angle her boots sideways to make them fit down the hole. A few wriggles later, her lower body is below the surface. The friction of the caving suit makes her cling to the sides of the rock and she has to keep wiggling to slide further down. It really is narrow.

Progress slows and her heart beats faster. She puts her arms straight up to make her shoulders as slim as possible. Every lump of rock scrapes against her body while she disappears from the surface, inch by inch. Then the passage widens, leaving her legs to move freely in the empty space. It frightens her until the harness carries her weight. Someone feeds a helmet through the opening. She puts it on and switches on the head torch.

The light reveals cobwebs and slimy algae. Below her are two glowing eyes. A blur of fur darts away. Looks too small for a dog. A rat? She calls to the surface to lower her further down.

Above ground, the old man picks up courage and hobbles towards the group for a better view. A wiry chap wearing builder's-trousers is lying on his front peering down a tiny hole. *Silence!* he shouts, just as a pair of delicate hands disappear down below. A minute goes by, everyone standing still in anticipation. Another rescuer, in camouflage trousers, leans towards the old man. *This might be the one,* he whispers.

Shall I brace myself for bad news, the old man asks.

No, no, she's probably alive. Done a few of these. They bounce remarkably well, dogs do. Not had a dead one yet. The rescuer seems so matter-of-fact. But, as they watch the ropes unravel, it becomes apparent just how deep the hole is.

The man on the ground shouts something down the void and waits for a reply. He looks up at the crowd and smiles when he spots the old man. *Looks like we've found Ruby.* The news is met by a cheer.

The old man's eyes fill with tears. The chap standing next to him puts his arms across his shoulders, which makes him cry even more. Sobs of relief, gratitude and tiredness. A canvas duffle bag is tied to a rope and pushed down the hole.

The camera is pointing at the hole. People remain silent as the bag is pulled to the surface and untied from the rope. A team member peers inside it before she puts it down by the old man's feet. He drops to his knees, even though he might not be able to get up again. Ruby's face pops out, soaking wet and covered in mud. She wags her tail so hard the whole bag wobbles as she licks the tears off his cheeks. The fellow next to him works hard to hold back his own tears.

Someone checks Ruby over but finds no injuries. Another team member wraps her in a towel and offers to carry her back to his car. As they leave, the old man gets a glimpse of the small lady getting changed. He ought to thank her, but now would not be a good time. He'll write a letter, yes, that's what he'll do. The phone rings.

Dad, it's me. Sorry, I couldn't talk yesterday.

In the background, the rescue leader is being interviewed by the ginger beard. Team members are packing away ladders and ropes.

What's going on? Is everything okay?
Yes, yes. Nothing to worry about. All is fine.

Dear Diary

21st March

Dear Diary,

Mum dragged me and Olivia around all the outdoor shops today. Lucky Charlie didn't spot me because I'm sure Mum would have said something really embarrassing. Why can't I have a normal mum like everyone else's?

Apparently, it's okay to go and buy stuff straight away if Mum needs something. When I want something, I have to wait until Christmas, even if I really need it. Not fair! Why does she suddenly need a backpack anyway?

She also tried on walking boots even though she already has three pairs. She didn't buy any though. Probably worried that Dad would moan and start calling her Imelda again. Mum doesn't like it but I quite like Imelda, it's a nice name.

She also bought a fleece jumper, a compass and a beanie with a big red bobble. Me and Olivia had to promise not to tell Dad how much she'd spent. Mum said the stuff she bought would help people in need, but

Dad might not understand. I don't know what she meant either. Is she going to post it to Syria or something?

25th March

Dear Diary,

Dad just told me that Mum's joining a mountain rescue team which explains why she went shopping for outdoor stuff last weekend. For some weird reason, she was selected when they were looking for new members.

She is not a climber or anything. 'It's not always about rope work, you know. Most of the time you just carry a stretcher,' she told me. I hope no one at school finds out.

'If you're so good at carrying things, why do you always get Dad to do it?' I asked her.

'To make him feel useful,' she replied.

Like Dad's not useful already! He makes pancakes every Saturday morning and hoovers the stairs. He's also way better at throwing Rafa's dog toys so they don't end up stuck in trees.

Mum also said you need to be good at finding missing people, so I can see why they want her in their team. She is really good at finding things. Me and Dad don't even try looking, it's much faster to ask Mum.

12th April

Dear Diary,

I got back from school today and found Mum hanging upside down off the bannister. She was practising abseiling but got the ropes tangled. I phoned Dad to tell him he needed to come home from work and video-streamed Mum to show him why. She kept shouting that I'd better not post that video on YouTube. Yeah, like I'd want anyone to know what a weirdo she is! No thanks! Dad fell off his office chair because he laughed so much.

Before I went to bed, she showed me how to tie a figure-of-eight knot, which was actually quite cool. I might show Charlie tomorrow at school.

1st June

Dear Diary,

This half-term holiday was the worst ever. It was even worse than going to school. Dad couldn't get time off work so Mum stayed at home to look after me and Olivia. Every day this week we had to go for walks, even when it rained. Only Rafa liked it, until Mum lost all his dog toys.

Mum made us count our steps. Olivia is only six, so she takes more steps than anyone else. Rafa takes either lots of little steps or just a few huge ones depending on how excited he is and because he is a spaniel he is almost always excited.

I now know that to walk 100m, I need to take 85 steps with my left leg. Not sure why it's important to know this, but Mum told me to remember it.

Most of the time we had to be quiet and not speak because Mum was busy counting. When she wasn't counting, she would stop and hold the map out in different directions, fiddling with the compass. I said, 'There's an app for this. Charlie showed me at school.'

'You might not have a phone with you,' she replied.

I said I was more likely to have a phone with me than a compass. She told me not to be a smart-arse.

Yesterday, Olivia and I were out again, this time with Dad. Mum told us to hide and message her our grid references so she could practice finding us. That's what people in mountain rescue do all the time apparently. After waiting for an hour behind a large rock, we gave up because it started raining again and Olivia was so cold she was shaking. Dad phoned Mum, but the call went straight to voicemail so she must have gone somewhere where there wasn't any signal. So we went home.

Two hours later, Mum came back, very angry. She said Dad had given her the grid references in the wrong order and she'd searched in the wrong place for hours.

Dad said he hadn't. But then he cooked dinner and I overheard him say he'd give her a foot massage later. He only does that when he's done something wrong.

To make matters worse, I hung my raincoat above my school shoes in the hallway, so this morning, the left shoe was soaking wet, but I had to wear it for school anyway.

23rd July

Dear Diary,

I'm hiding in my bedroom. Mum and Dad are shouting at each other. It started on the way home from Nanna's. Mum had taken Dad along to today's rescue team practice so he could pretend to be a casualty. I said I'd do it, but they aren't allowed to use children anymore.

In the car on the way home, she laughed and told me and Olivia how the team had joked about having to practise with a 'heavy load'. Dad thought she meant that the team had called him fat, and that it wasn't funny. The thing is, Dad is fat. His belly hangs over his trousers and you can even see the skin of his stomach between the shirt buttons when he sits down. He said he'd never offer to help again. That's fine by me because it's boring to be at Nanna's. I miss my Playstation and all we do is jigsaws and drawing, which is what Olivia likes.

Charlie and Ellie found out that Mum has joined the rescue team. Surprisingly, they seemed to think that was pretty cool. I just hope Mum doesn't annoy the team like she annoys everyone at home.

13th September

Dear Diary,

Today my teacher phoned Mum at work to complain about the used bandage I had brought to school yesterday. Mr Honeydew said it was a health hazard and that my mother was totally irresponsible giving it to me.

Mum didn't know what my teacher was talking about until she got home and I told her that I found a bandage covered in blood in her team jacket and that I wanted to show it to my friends. I'd made up a story about Mum saving an old man who had fallen from a cliff and how the bandage had blown off him when the helicopter landed.

'It wasn't quite like that,' she said and laughed. 'I slipped on the greasy path outside the rescue base last Wednesday and scraped my elbow.' She rolled up her sleeve and showed me her scab.

2nd November

Dear Diary,

This half-term has been really cool because Mum took me and Olivia caving. She found out about the cave because they practised rescuing someone on a special stretcher through lots of narrow tunnels. She told me not to tell Dad that everyone had been happy that he hadn't volunteered to be the casualty.

Because Olivia is tiny, she is the fastest at crawling, but she cried when her wellies filled up with cold water. The water was the coldest I have ever felt, but since Olivia was crying, I had to pretend it wasn't cold even though my feet had turned white by the time we got back to the surface.

Mum said that sometimes it takes weeks to rescue someone from a cave because it is very difficult. I think they should practise it a bit more because it sounds like they are not very good at it.

26th December

Dear Diary,

Mum claimed Father Christmas is a member of the mountain rescue team and that's why Olivia, Dad, Nanna, Grandma and I received mountain rescue neck buffs for Christmas this year. I know Father Christmas isn't real but couldn't say anything as it would have upset Olivia. I suppose he does wear a red jacket… In any case, if I break my leg, I'm going to wish that I get rescued by Father Christmas (and not Mum).

4th March

Dear Diary,

Today Oliva and I were locked in our Volvo in the car park at Aysgarth Falls. We had stopped for ice cream when two mountain rescue Land Rovers appeared. They all knew Mum and asked her to help them look for this old demented lady, even though she's not yet a "proper" team member. We waited in the car and pretended that we were dogs, panting heavily every time anyone walked past. Well, at least until an old man said he'd smash the window to let us out. We quickly opened the door, explaining that Mum would be back soon. Still, he didn't leave.

When Mum came back, she couldn't find the car key so everyone had to go and search for it, while the angry man kept staring at us. She then found it inside the top pocket of her backpack. She blamed it on 'men-of-paws'. I'm not sure why 'men' need to be blamed. Seems a bit unfair, but then Dad gets blamed for everything these days, so I suppose it makes sense.

The old lady who was missing had been found in a cafe drinking a cup of tea. She had forgotten to tell anyone where she was going. I can see now why Mum always wants me to tell her where I'm going. I wouldn't want lots of police and mountain rescuers to have to search for me if I'm late home for dinner.

23rd May

Dear Diary,

Me, Olivia and Dad stayed with Grandma and Grandad this weekend. Mum didn't want to come with us because on Friday she finished her mountain rescue training and now she can go on proper rescues. Dad moaned about her always finding an excuse every time his parents invite us over. I like going to Grandma and Grandpa's because they live close to the beach. Me and Olivia played 'I spy' in the car both there and back.

When we got home there was a big fire engine outside our house. The downstairs was full of smoke. Dad was really worried at first but laughed when Mum said she'd had her first callout and had rushed off in a panic. The pizza she'd left in the oven looked like a black frisbee. Apparently, she didn't have to do anything because the injured person had already left before she got there. It's a shame because I would have liked to tell Charlie about it.

24th June

Dear Diary,

Today Mum was on the telly! But first I need to write about Rafa. He's a very clever dog because he knows when Mum needs to go on a callout. He can recognize the special sound her phone makes and goes straight into his crate! He is much cleverer than the spaniel on the telly today. It had fallen into a hole on the moor. The hole was so narrow nobody could get him up until they asked my Mum to do it. My mum! I can't believe it! The TV crew filmed as they tied a rope to her and she managed to wiggle down. At one point only her hands were sticking out above the ground. When they pulled up the rope, there was a bag tied to the other end, and inside was a very wet doggie. Lots of people cried because they were so happy to see it.

I can't wait to tell my friends at school tomorrow.

They must have pulled Mum up too because she tucked me into bed this evening.

'I didn't know that mountain rescue rescued dogs,' I said.

'Yes, we'll rescue all kinds of animals,' she replied.

'Even a tiger?'

'Maybe even a tiger.'

I've got the coolest mum ever!

Dead Still

The stillness confuses the small spaniel as she nuzzles up to the limp hand of the old gentleman, his body splayed on the soft moorland heather. She licks his fingers and expects a stroke, but none is forthcoming. She tries again; someone shouts. She is dragged away, but tugs hard on the lead to try and get a glimpse of her best friend.

*

A broad-shouldered gamekeeper drops to his knees next to the lifeless man, shakes his shoulders and puts his ear against a pale face. Feeling, listening, hoping. The wind is too strong to detect any breathing. He removes his thick gloves and unzips the gentleman's coat, revealing a creased neck with several shaving cuts. The Keeper buries his bulky fingers deep, desperate to feel a heartbeat. He keeps trying. Deep down, he knows. The man is so still.

    The Keeper drops his head and tries to figure out what to do next. It's his shoot, his people doing the beating, and it's his responsibility that the guns, who have paid handsomely to shoot grouse, have a good time. He calls out, attracting the attention of the other beaters. They change course and are soon gathered around him, shock written across their flushed faces. It was only a minute since the old man was one of them, fighting the terrain to get across the moor. They are still holding the large plastic flags that they were cracking to scare the grouse out of the deep heather. Shots are still being fired as straggling birds fly over the butts not far away. Someone calls an ambulance.

A woman in dark blue waterproofs kneels down and repeats the checks for breathing and pulse. She unwraps the man from his clothing to reveal a large white belly, like a well-proven dough with a slight wobble. The movement is strangely comforting. Leaning over his chest and, with her arms perfectly straight, she starts giving chest compressions. Every fifteen seconds or so, she stops, positions the old man's head between her hands, covers his mouth with hers and blows two steady breaths into his lungs. The remaining beaters stare at the stomach that expands and then contracts, just as if he were still alive. They all suspect it's in vain, but feel reassured that someone is doing something.

The Keeper sounds his horn for the guns to stop shooting.

*

Not a bad result. The Gun nods to his loader as he hands him his shotgun. They wait in anticipation of the signal to release the dogs to pick up the fallen grouse, but the beaters aren't coming any closer. They all seem to be heading left, towards a spot on the tall bank in front of the grouse butts. Their movements are jerky and cumbersome; the ground is unforgiving. Something isn't right. The Gun leaves his butt and joins a small group of jolly shooters. His black labrador picks up a bird and wags his tail as he carries its tiny corpse softly in his mouth. Loaders start clearing away the empty cartridges. Now and again they glance at the group on the slope above.

A message comes over the radio. They need a doctor. The Gun straightens his back and announces with a deep voice that he's happy to help. One of the keepers leads him up towards the group in the distance. He gets out of breath quickly, not used to the terrain, and stops to unbutton his dark green shooting jacket and put his flat cap in his pocket. The heather is knee-high and clings to his tweed breeks. It takes them over five minutes to climb the hill.

He notices a figure performing chest compressions and his heart sinks. He knows the statistics. Out here, on the moor, no chance. The face of the man lying on the ground is tinged purple. His mouth is wide open, and his lips have receded to reveal his teeth, making him look angry. The Gun can't help but admire the lady as she puts her lips against the dead man's mouth and blows.

He lets everyone know he's a doctor, asks what's happened and then tells the lady to stop the compressions. He observes the man's chest for movement and then rules out the presence of a pulse. Without the woman's efforts to pump life into the body, it has regained its eerie stillness. The beaters - an unstylish bunch of teenagers, a couple of old men in dark green coats and some thin-looking ladies, well-preserved for their age - are no longer on their guard. A few sit down on their haunches, facing away now there's nothing more to be done.

Where the sun breaks through the clouds, bursts of yellow and vivid purple light up the otherwise grey moors. He scans the soft remote hills, not a proper road in sight. The nearest hospital is easily an hour and a half away. He's startled when a grouse takes off from the heather only a few metres away. He sighs. He was shooting well today. A procession of guns is slowly making their way over, curious and impatient. Soon they are gathered around the deceased. *Terrible. Awful. Is an ambulance coming? Do we know the gentleman? No? A flanker, did you say? How unfortunate.*

They all pretend to want the shooting day to be cancelled, forfeiting the large amount they have paid for the privilege, not to mention the cost of travel and accommodation. Of course, it would be inappropriate to leave one of the underkeepers here waiting for the ambulance, while they carried on to the next drive. Or would it not?

Nobody is crouching down by the body anymore. Standing up, they can pretend he's not there. The conversation drifts towards more mundane topics and the beaters start unwrapping their sandwiches. Occasionally, they throw a glance towards the dead gentleman, his mouth still wide open, eyes staring at the sky and his belly exposed to the wind.

Someone shouts and everyone's attention is on the bright yellow dot on the horizon. An ambulance is crawling up the narrow track, blue lights flashing.

*

The Paramedic points towards a dark green terrain vehicle and tells her colleague to drive towards it. Soon they are following the Kawasaki Mule, accompanied by the brushing sound of the tall grass in the middle of the track that's polishing their undercarriage. Every bump is making their expensive equipment tremble. Eighty-year-old male. Cardiac arrest. Standard - but inconvenient. She glances at the side mirror; a police van has caught up with them. You can't be too careful with a death on a grouse shoot.

The terrain becomes too rough and they stop and turn the engine off. A few hundred metres away, there is a group of people, a couple of them are waving. An underkeeper gives her a lift to the casualty site, her heavy bags deposited on top of braces of newly shot grouse stacked neatly in the open cargo area at the back. Her uniform isn't enough to keep her warm, not up here. The strong wind is making the right side of her face ache.

When she arrives, the bystanders are keen to unburden themselves of responsibility. While listening, she looks at the deceased. His face is now blue, as are his hands. There's no doubt that he's passed, but still, she goes through the protocol - no breathing, no pulse. She attaches a monitor to the man's chest to be certain. For the second time that day, she declares another human dead. Life extinct, only the shell remains. The dead body doesn't worry her, but the distance between it and the ambulance does. Should she ask for mountain rescue? It would add another hour or two to the job. Her thoughts are interrupted by a young police officer tapping her shoulder.

She moves back to let the officer gain access. He looks like a kid in a fancy dress costume, his fluorescent yellow jacket forming a tent around him as he crouches down. There are no holes in the semi-naked gentleman's front or his back; that's all they ever check for. Boxes ticked, notes taken.

She pulls out a body bag from her medical pack and opens the zip all the way around. The wind nearly rips the white plastic sheet out of her hands. Everyone is keen to help and they gather the corners and help her feed the sheet underneath the old man. It is only when the zip is pulled up along the sides they realise how tall he is. There isn't enough bag left to fully cover his head. Someone suggests removing his boots. All eyes are on her as they pause for a decision. She asks the person next to her to lift the top of the bag slightly. The body slumps and there's enough slack to close the zip. The conversation is starting to flow now the gentleman is covered in plastic. Plans are being made, decisions taken on which pub to meet up in, to compensate for their spoilt afternoon no doubt. Out of sight - out of mind. She can't argue with that. It's how she keeps going.

The police officer tells her that a keeper has offered the use of the Mule to help with transport. At first, she imagines the corpse propped up on the seat next to the driver, but the officer is pointing to the back of the vehicle. Relieved, she gives the nod. Soon the white bag is on top of the fluffy bodies of the birds, like another hunting trophy. A couple of beaters volunteer to support the legs that hang over the edge of the cargo area to make sure the body doesn't slip off. They begin the journey down the hill, towards the ambulance, where her colleague is waiting with a trolley. Everyone else follows behind, pleased to be able to move from the patch of moorland where they have spent the last couple of hours.

*

The guns pile into their black Range Rovers, the beaters are ushered into ex-Army trucks and the cortege follows the ambulance as it makes its way off the moor. A funeral procession, one man and twenty braces of grouse being the morning's casualties.

The Paramedic laughs as she describes her last blind date to her colleague. The Gun curses as he discovers his cap has fallen out of his coat pocket. The Keeper worries that the Lord of the Manor will disapprove of him cancelling the two remaining drives. The dog is whimpering in the back of the truck with the beaters, confused, his master's seat is empty.

In the distance, grouse butts are visible like dark dots punctuating the landscape, marking the boundary of life and death for thousands of birds over the years. The butts are made from heavy wooden logs and are half sunk into the ground, like immovable bastions of death, but yet, they are not as still as a dead body.

('Dead Still' was published in the Parracombe Prize 2023 Anthology)

First Time

'Be organised,' they've told me. 'Make sure everything is packed and ready.'

That's okay. 'Organised' is my middle name. I've emptied the contents of my backpack on the dining table. Just to make sure it's all there. The orange helmet. The harness with the shiny new climbing gear attached. A small group shelter, to protect the casualty from the elements. A pair of spare gloves and a hat, a torch, a first aid kit, sunscreen, mosquito repellent, a compass, a couple of maps, and ten metres of rope. I glance at the radio that's sitting on the charging station. In an hour or so it should be fully charged. I pack everything away again and add a small notepad and a pen, which I even remember to test to ensure it works. Attention to detail is everything.

It's a sunny Saturday morning in late May. My husband and children are visiting the grandparents at the seaside while I've managed to wiggle out of the trip on the basis that it's my first weekend as a fully-fledged mountain rescue team member.

Cars speed through the village, taking tourists up the valley. From the kitchen window, I see walkers heading out across the lush green hills, like a sparse trail of ants. While they are out enjoying the sunshine, I'm too nervous to leave my house, just in case a call comes through. The mobile signal is weak and patchy in our valley so I have my phone propped up against the window in the living room, the best spot for reliable reception, and I dare not move it.

I pace from the living room to the kitchen and back, fluffing the sofa cushions and dusting the window sills. I make another cup of tea. The phone beeps. My heart jumps. I jump. It's not a callout, just hubby saying they've arrived in Formby.

The day goes by. I do nothing in particular. My phone is unusually quiet so I check that the battery isn't flat or that I've accidentally switched on aeroplane mode. I have a fitful night's sleep.

The next day it rains so I feel less guilty staying indoors. Still waiting. Still hoping. It's not like I wish someone would hurt themselves. Actually, I'll be blunt about it, I do. Nothing serious of course. If it's going to happen, let it happen today, when I'm available and ready. Maybe someone could get slightly lost or a dog could fall down a hole. No, not the dog, definitely not the dog. Have I become a psychopath? I shudder. To stop worrying about my mental state I start reading a book about camels in the Kalahari desert, but after an hour I'm still on page five.

At six o'clock on Sunday night, I give up. We're not going to get called out this weekend. By now, people will have made it home, safe and sound. An orange sun has appeared, making the stone walls cast dark shadows across the glowing fields. Soon hubby and kids will return. 'Don't worry about dinner,' he'd said. 'Grandma will make sure we leave with full bellies.'

I put a frozen ham and pineapple pizza in the oven.

For the first time in two days I relax. I realise I stink from all that nervous energy so take off the hiking clothes I've been wearing all weekend and throw them in the washing basket. I have fifteen minutes before the pizza is ready.

While in the shower, my thoughts are suddenly free to wander, to the appointment at the dentist the next day, to booking the cat in with the vet for vaccinations, to the damp patch on the spare bedroom ceiling. By the time I step out of the shower, a callout is the last thing on my mind.

Beep beep… It's my phone. A message.

In my rush to grab a towel from the towel rail, I slip on the wet floor and hit my face on the toilet seat. Blood marks my route to the living room. I press some scrunched up toilet tissue against my throbbing nose preparing to be disappointed. It's bound to be my husband letting me know they're going to be late. But no, it's a callout, a proper one. A girl has fallen off a cliff. Near the river. Caller intoxicated. Full team callout.

I'm not organised, I'm naked and still bleeding. A hasty return to the bathroom. Smelly clothes fished out of the washing basket. I have one leg through my trousers when I realise I haven't responded to the message. I attempt to put the other leg in while hopping across the living room. I knock over a plant, the ceramic pot breaking into sharp fragments on the stone floor. And the blood keeps dripping. Yes, I'm attending. I'm very much attending.

I grab my bag and leave the house, returning once to pick up the car keys, then go back again because I've forgotten the radio and a final time because I need the toiley, desperately. I've been told adrenalin can have that effect.

I pull out of the drive while congratulating myself on only taking seven minutes to get rolling, before I'm forced to pull over as I have no idea where I'm going. By now there are more messages on my phone. I spot a grid reference and get the map out, its sheer size filling every window as I struggle to find the right coordinates. I get annoyed when a passing tourist knocks on the window asking if I need directions.

Turns out the road down the valley is closed and I have to take a twenty-minute detour stuck behind a tractor doing fifteen miles per hour. By the time I get to the rendezvous, there are already fifteen team members on the scene and I get told that the casualty has self-rescued. She's been checked over by a paramedic and returned to her party. There is nothing for the team to do. After the stand-down message, the team disperses, and I flop into the driver's seat, like a melted crash dummy, hardly able to move a finger. I spot my messed up face in the rearview mirror and realise why everyone was staring at me.

The adrenaline fades as I slowly make my way home. A fire engine overtakes me, but I hardly notice. When I arrive home, I'm shocked to see it parked outside my cottage with its blue lights flashing. Evil tendrils of dark smoke drift from gaps in the kitchen window. The firefighters stand ready to knock my door down while the neighbours have lined up to watch. They are shivering with their arms crossed, unwilling to go back home and put something warmer on in case they miss something. I run past the crowd shouting. 'Stop! I've got a key!' This is the moment my husband and children arrive home.

Later that evening, my husband smirks at me. 'You got a call out then?' The kids are in bed and I have wiped the blood off the floor, the rugs, the sofa, the window sills and the bathroom and cleaned up the broken pot and damp soil from the house plant. Every window is open to try and get rid of the smell of burnt pizza.

'This isn't what it's going to be like every time, is it?'

I shake my head. 'No, next time I'll be more organised.'

I Had Just…

I had just taken the first mouthful of my dinner…

I had just got to the front of the queue at the post office…

I had just gone to sleep…

I had just mixed a bucket of mortar…

I had just given my wife a bunch of flowers…

I had just ordered a delivery pizza…

I had just filled my trolley at the supermarket…

I had just stepped into the shower…

I had just arrived at my sister-in-law's 50th birthday party…

I had just been told my Dad had passed away…

…when the message came: Female, 70s, slipped on rocks, suspected broken hip at Aysgarth Falls.

Bodies in the Water

'Mummy, look! A naked lady.' The little girl wearing red wellies clings to the metal railing that separates the park from the fast-flowing water. She points to something floating down the river. 'Look, Mummy! Look!'

The little girl's mother sits on a bench nearby, scrolling on her phone.

'What, sweetie?'

'A lady in the water.' The girl follows the woman with her finger. The mother only looks up when it's too late.

'What did you see, sweetie?' she asks.

'A naked lady. She's gone now.' The girl sighs and kicks a pebble into the water.

'Oh, what a shame. Come on, time to pick your brother up from school.'

The girl grabs her mother's hand, skipping towards the road, her lively, blue eyes still glued to the river.

Maureen, 62, *Local dog walker*
Of course, I looked at them. How could I not? Lying there by the river, their bits exposed to the sun. Shocking! Those women showed complete inconsideration towards decent god-fearing people. Not even the slightest bit bothered that children were playing close by. What would have happened if they had spotted them? Doesn't bear thinking about. Of course, I phoned the police. Someone has to make sure good morals are upheld.

Gordon, 68, *Mountain rescue controller*
The first message from the police came at 14:45. Body spotted in the River Swale, downstream of Station Bridge. It's the fastest river in England, you know. Not many people know that. We alerted the team requesting swiftwater technicians to get moving. By 15:00 we couldn't keep up with the messages. That's when we knew it was a major incident.

Gary, 59, *Mountain rescue volunteer*
I've never experienced anything like yesterday. We've had multiple callouts in one day, sometimes quite close together, but seventy-three in two hours. Unbelievable. I didn't know what to do other than stay in the car and scroll through the incoming messages.

Sarah, 44, *Mountain rescue training officer*
This is what we train for. In some ways it resembled our training sessions, just with more casualties. A lot more. Obviously, it helped that none of them were alive.

Tom, 21, *Mountain rescue volunteer*
I was by the river picking litter with the Keep Swaledale Clean group when I spotted a body in the river. I phoned the police and told them to call out mountain rescue. That's how it's supposed to be done. We aren't allowed to respond to a rescue unless instructed by the police or ambulance service to do so. I then told them that they were speaking to mountain rescue already. I know I don't look or sound old enough to be a member, but I am. They didn't believe me so I hung up. I probably confused them, to be honest.

Beth, 39, *Emergency call handler*
Yes, that was easily the busiest day in a long time. What was the first call? I'm trying to think. There was a call from someone saying there was a body in the river, who sounded to be about twelve years old. They claimed they were a member of the local mountain rescue team. This person was so incoherent I suspected it was a prank, especially when they just hung up. After that, all hell broke loose. Initially, we dispatched teams to each sighting, but quickly ran out of officers. It was only when the call came in about the lorry, it all made sense.

Lukasz, 29, *Lorry driver*
I was afraid for my own skin. I don't know what happened. Narrow road, satnav. When I look up, my lorry was falling. From high up and down into the water. I don't know. Not predictable. I mean not preventable. No not right. More like, surprise to me. Big surprise to me. I go out of lorry but river is so strong. Then I see bodies. So many. All naked. I thought, no can't be true. No refugees on my lorry, not possible. But I saw with own eyes, so many peoples. I got to side of water and I run into the woods. I think I might be in big trouble.

Penny, 45, *Richmond Gazette*
The first I knew about it was when I saw all the police vans everywhere with their blue lights on. It's like porn for a journalist. They were followed by the fire engines and a handful of ambulances. They were going in all directions like they didn't know where to start. I got so excited I started hyperventilating, nearly falling off my bike. A minute or so later my phone started ringing.

    The first caller was quite aggressive. Asked why the yellow duck race had been replaced by some fetish sex doll race, and could they get the details of the organiser. I didn't make the connection then, as I was in pursuit of a police van and didn't have the faintest idea what was going on. I knew it was big though, very big.

Jim, 72, *Mountain rescue volunteer*
What water job? I dropped my phone in Graham's slurry pit on Friday. No one said anything about it in the pub yesterday. You sure it's real?

Keith, *age undisclosed, Mountain rescue equipment officer*
I was first on the scene in Richmond. Actually, I was in the scene, swimming in a calm section of the river, training for an Iron Man competition, when police officers and firemen on the bank started shouting at me. They then threw a line for me to grab. I didn't want to seem ungrateful so I held on to it to let them pull me ashore.

    I thanked them and said I was a member of the mountain rescue team. Did they need my help? They looked surprised and asked me if by any chance I'd seen a Polish lorry driver. I said no, and went back to doing lengths up and down the river promising to look out for him.

    Did I see anything unusual? Yes, there had been a higher-than-average number of wild swimmers, you know, menopausal ladies needing to cool off in cold water, that kind of thing. At least that's what I thought at the time. I don't wear glasses while swimming.

Neil, 48, *Rescue controller*

I can't tell you how relieved I was when the first mannequin was pulled out of the river. Together with Fire and Rescue and the Environmental Agency, we started pulling them out by the dozen, working our way along the banks. Sightings were reported as far downriver as Skipton-on-Swale, so it was a big job. We needed to get them out of the water, as otherwise the general public might think they were real and put themselves at risk trying to save them. I also had concerns they might cause a blockage further downstream.

After a couple of hours, there were piles of them stacked up everywhere. Quite gross to be honest. We noticed lots of them being carried off by youths and shop assistants since we didn't have enough people to guard them once they were out of the water.

A couple of times we were called to specific locations as they thought they had located the driver, but each time it was a false alarm. We kept looking, but if he was unconscious or deceased, the water could have pulled his clothes off and he would have been difficult to distinguish from the plastic figures.

At 16:55 we got a message saying that a person was hanging from a tree, down from Round Howe Woods. Usually, people found hanging in trees have been quite determined to put themselves there in the first place. However, the police then added that the person was calling for help which immediately cheered us up. I dispatched a group of team members to assist.

Craig, 39, *Mountain rescue volunteer (surface rescue only)*
We heard the casualty shouting and had to traverse a particularly steep and muddy section of woodland to locate him. He was hanging off a branch that had caught his jacket and suspended him in the air during his efforts to get away from the riverbank. His clothes were dripping wet, so we suspected that we'd found the driver. He was reluctant to admit it at first and only confessed after we pretended we were leaving him up there, even though we were only going to go back to the vehicle to get our ropes and rigging kit.

Chantal, 24, *Shop assistant (Ladies' wear), Slough*
We'd been lookin' for mannequins for months. Second hand of course. Even them ones are super expensive! Imagine how chuffed I was when forty-five of 'em was listed dead cheap on eBay. Bought five for forty quid and I'm gonna collect them from Richmond this afternoon. What do you mean there are two Richmonds? Where's the second one? North Yorkshire? You've got to be taking the piss, that's like miles and miles away!

*

A torso is bobbing up and down on the waves with a seagull perched on a nippleless breast. The left arm is lying on the bank next to the caravan site in Topcliffe, the right one is stuck behind a tree branch overhanging the river next to the Millenium Bridge in York. The left leg was picked up by a soldier as it floated past RAF Leeming and is now lying under his bed in the barrack. The right leg was knocked off in the Humber by a Finnish cargo ship delivering paper envelopes. The little girl in green wellies has spotted the head lodged between two large rocks at Richmond Falls and points it out to her brother.

The torso drifts to the middle of the North Sea. In a week, a helicopter from the Netherlands's Coastguard will be dispatched to investigate the sightings reported by a retired primary school teacher on board the P&O ferry Pride of Rotterdam.

Under Ground

The light from my headtorch is reflected in the water that forty minutes ago wasn't there. Now it is blocking our route out of the cave. The thought of squeezing through it with one gulp of air to last God knows how long, terrifies me beyond belief. I pray that isn't Ryan's plan. He's so close behind me in the passage that I can feel his breath on my neck.

'Did you tell Nicole where you were going tonight?' I ask.

'She knows I'm caving. Didn't tell her where though.'

'Great… So no one knows where we are?' I knew it. It's like those Thai boys. How long were they trapped for? Two weeks? But people knew they were down there. The whole world knew. 'Someone will come for us, won't they?'

Ryan turns around and begins to crawl on his elbows deeper into the mountain.

'Where're you going?' I ask. 'Is there another exit?'

'Not that I'm aware of, but it slopes upwards at least.'

'So, it will take a bit longer for us to drown? Holy shit, some date you've taken me on.'

All I can hear is the scraping of Ryan's caving suit against the rough rock until he turns around and shouts, 'It shouldn't rise much higher.'

'But what if it does?'

I follow with sore elbows. My wellies are full of freezing water. The helmet Ryan has lent me is too big and keeps tipping onto the bridge of my nose, like it's trying to chop it off. I'm not used to this. Two hours ago, I'd pulled a newly purchased caving suit out of its plastic packaging.

We stop in a section of the passage which is nearly a metre in height, sitting with our backs against the wall and feet resting on the opposite side. It's too narrow to stretch our legs, but at least we're able to sit straight without bending our necks. I rub my left elbow.

'Did you not look out of the window this afternoon?' I ask. 'Never mind cats and dogs, it was more like elephants!'

'This cave isn't supposed to be wet,' Ryan answers.

'Looks wet to me. I can't believe you talked me into this.' I wrap my arms around my legs to keep warm. I'm irritated at his calmness.

'You didn't tell anyone then?' he asks.

'Of course not! You told me not to. Said people would put two and two together, remember? So, what will Nicole do if you don't come home tonight?'

'How am I supposed to know?'

'You're the one married to her.'

'I guess she'll call 999.'

'What if she finds out? About us, I mean?

I notice that Ryan's face hardens. Here we go again. Whenever I mention our relationship, he turns sour. Or is it the rising water that's beginning to worry him?

'I'll think of something. Anyway, I'm going to check on the water level. I'm sure it'll start dropping soon.'

'Don't tell me it's still rising. Oh fuck, it is, isn't it? I can't believe it,' I say when Ryan reappears. I blind him with my torch and he puts his hand up to shield his eyes. He frowns.

'Sorry.' I mumble and aim the light above our heads where fat drops of water are clinging on to a few stalactites.

'It's not rising very fast.'

I'm cross but don't want to show it. I'm not sure what to say. It's been ages since we were able to have an evening together and now this.

'Why'd you wanna come down here?' I ask.

'I'm taking Nicole's sister underground next weekend. Just wanted to check if there were any tight squeezes.'

'You mean if her breasts will fit. I know Jessica.' I look away as soon as I've said it. I had sounded jealous. 'I didn't have Jessica down as a caver, that's all.'

We sit in awkward silence. I want to change the topic, to sound cheerful and accommodating, but my mind is blank.

Ryan breaks the silence. 'We need to switch off our torches to save the batteries.'

For a few seconds, the light from Ryan's torch stays imprinted on my retina, after that it's dark. Completely dark. Like we've been buried alive.

'Your teeth are chattering,' Ryan says like I wasn't already aware of it.

'I'm cold.'

'Try moving around.'

'Don't tell me what I should do. It's all your fault.'

'No, I mean it.' Ryan touches my arm. 'Let's go and check the water. We'll use your torch, mine's nearly out of charge.'

'It's about the same as before,' Ryan says and lets me slide up next to him.

I peer into the passage and for a moment I think someone is coming to help us, but it's just the water reflecting the bright light from my torch.

'If Nicole calls the police, what will happen?' I ask.

'I guess they'll call the cave rescue team. At some point, they'll find my car. I'd imagine they'll wait until the water drops a bit before they go in.'

'We could be dead by then.'

'Stop worrying, the water will drop as quickly as it rose, once it stops raining.'

I can tell Ryan is tense. He refuses to look at me. Or maybe he's just worried I'm going to blind him again.

'So, you didn't look at the forecast then?' I ask.

'Not in detail, no.'

'It's gonna rain pretty much solidly for the next three days.' I wait for Ryan to say something but he seems focused on scraping mud off his gloves. After a few minutes, we crawl back to where we were earlier and sit in the dark without speaking.

'How long has it been now?' I ask and switch the torch on so that Ryan can look at his watch. I'm hungry and cold.

'Five hours.'

'They'll definitely be looking for us now, right?' I snuggle up against him for comfort. 'Come on. Let's kiss. Might as well.'

Ryan recoils the moment I slide my hand down the front of his caving suit finding his warm armpit. 'Whoa, keep those cold hands to yourself.'

I tilt my helmet back so I can put my lips against his. He's not leaning in, and I can tell his mind is somewhere else. I suppress a sigh, lean back against the rock and hold his cold glove in mine. 'Just imagine, we could have gone to the shooting hut. Or Leeds.' I switch the torch off, plummeting us back into darkness. 'When can you get away again?'

'It's a bit tricky at the moment.'

'It's been a month since we had proper time together. I'm not gonna count tonight, even if we're stuck here until tomorrow.'

'I'll arrange something soon, promise.'

'You remember what you said this time last year? You said we'd be living together by now. Remember? Maybe this is a sign?' It's the first time I've brought it up since he promised that he'd leave Nicole, even though it had constantly been on my mind.

'It's not that easy.'

'Isn't it? I'm sick of pretending to be single, you know.'

'I know. Not sure Nicole would cope very well. I just need a bit more time.'

I breathe in sharply and let the air out slowly through my nose to stay calm. I don't want to cry. I don't want to be here. I don't want to say anything but something snaps inside me. 'It's all about Nicole! First, you said we had to wait until your daughter had gone to uni, and now what? What are we waiting for now? Nicole to die, so you don't have to feel guilty? You said you don't love her anymore. You don't, do you? Oh, come on. You still love her? Really? Why are you here with me then?'

'I do love you, but–'

'Jesus Christ! Just don't expect me to lie when they find us. I'm done with covering for you. We should have had this conversation ages ago. If you knew the sacrifices I've made.'

'I'm sorry but... Where are you going?'

'I'm not sitting next to you. You and your 'buts'. I can't believe this. I really thought you were serious about us.' I feel my way across the sharp rocks scattered on the floor to get a bit of space between us.

'I was – I mean, I am... It's just–'

'*Just* is no better than *but*.'

'Oh, come on. Don't overreact. If we only–.'

'Don't talk to me.' I draw a deep breath and let the air out slowly through my mouth.

'We can do this. I just need a bit more time, that's all.'

'More time? You must be joking. I hate caving by the way. I only came along so I could see you. I'm glad this has happened so Nicole finds out. You know what? I'm telling her, as soon as we're out of here.'

'Alright then, I've been an arse, but—'

'I said no *buts*.'

'I'll figure something out.'

We sit and stare into the dark listening to drops of water falling from the stalactites.

'Give me your torch. I will go and check on the water level,' Ryan says as if he's been wanting to spit the words out for the last hour or so.

I pull the torch off my helmet and fumble with stiff hands for the 'on' switch. 'Shall I come? Not sure I wanna be left in the dark.'

'No, it's quicker if I go on my own. Need to save battery, remember?'

'You'll be back straight away, won't you?'

'Sure.'

'Promise?'

'Promise.'

Snowbound

Snow is falling, merging the sky with the moorland, turning the valley tops a desolate white. As the light fades, it settles on lower ground too, where dark stonewalls mark the boundary between the moor and the fields and connect the farms with the tracks. People struggle home, worried about getting stranded. Headlights from slow-moving cars join the villages along the valley bottom. Wipers work overtime to clear sticky snowflakes from the windscreens. The top of the moors are best avoided.

But there's a speck of light up there, all on its own; a BMW, front wheels stuck in a snow-filled ditch. The tyre marks would have shown a hasty attempt to turn around, but the whirling snow has already covered them.

Everything has been said, even the things that shouldn't be. *Stupid not to have left earlier… If only the Satnav hadn't… I did say… If you'd been more careful…*

In the driver's seat, sits the husband in his early forties with manicured stubble that hides the beginning of a double chin. He slams both hands on the steering wheel and shakes his head. His wife, in the passenger seat, holds a sleeping baby boy wrapped in a dog blanket. She stares at the snow-covered windscreen. Her blonde hair is a mess of curls, and she uses her sleeve to wipe tears from her eyes. Every few minutes she blows her nose in a scrunched-up tissue. On the backseat lies a brown Labrador, curled up to keep warm. He's uncomfortable with the silence and lifts his eyelids every time someone moves.

Their first weekend away for over a year, and neither of them got any sleep because the baby had been teething. Heavy rain for two days. Dog shitting on the hotel room carpet. And now this. The man flirts with the idea of storming off into the snow to leave it all behind. Get his old life back. The way he used to spend his free time: squash, restaurants, long weekends in Paris and New York. Not this. He sighs and gets his phone out. At least up here he has a signal, not like down in the valley.

He is on hold for a minute before he can explain where they are and what has happened, his voice heavy with frustration. He hangs up and looks at his wife. She refuses to meet his gaze. There are sharp lines either side of her mouth and her eyes are puffy. He can see the resemblance to her mother.

They say nothing, just wait while the wind howls and occasionally rocks the car. He thinks of the meeting he has scheduled with a client back in Manchester in the morning, about a contract worth millions. Big housing development on a brownfield site. He closes his eyes and leans back on the head rest.

The fuel gauge warning light comes on so he turns the ignition off, plunging them into darkness as the headlights go out. The temperature drops. It's been half-an-hour since he spoke to the police. His wife's teeth start to chatter while she strokes the face of the child. *Fuck, fuck, fuck*, he shouts.

Down in the valley, two mountain rescue Land Rovers set off from the depot. The first travels up the northern dale, while the other approaches from the south. They start climbing slushy roads to get to the top of the moor. The vehicle on the south side is forced to stop. Dark figures wearing head torches emerge and start shovelling to get past a drift, but soon hit another one. The other Land Rover carries on higher, wheels slipping but eventually finding traction. Soon they are also forced to stop, the snow is too deep. Four team members dressed in thick red coats with reflective markings head up the hill on foot, wading through the heavy snow. They hope they are on the right road as there are several crossing the moor, connecting the two valleys.

The Labrador barks sharply when bright lights penetrate the snow-covered windows. The baby starts to cry. The husband has to use his shoulder to open the door, a drift having built up against the side of the car. The icy wind sails through his wool jacket. His leather brogues sink deep into the snow, as he greets the small team that has come to their assistance. He shoves his bare hands in his trouser pockets and pulls his shoulders up high, while he explains how unlucky they were to end up here on a night like this. They're visiting for the weekend, now on their way home. He looks around for a vehicle that can tow him out. There isn't one. Could they give his car a push?

He is told that the car will stay where it is, they've only come to help him and his family to safety. Anything else, he'll have to arrange tomorrow. *Don't worry*, someone says, *the snow won't be around for long. It never is.*

The stranded family is asked to gather up their essentials. The husband opens the boot and pulls out a travel cot, a suitcase and a large shoulder bag and chucks them in the snow. He's angry with the weather, with his life and with how they'll be stranded in the Yorkshire Dales another night.

They're offered coats, which he declines without thinking. His wife, on the other hand, dons a large red jacket, big enough to also cover the baby. She apologises repeatedly for being an inconvenience. *Don't worry. We're happy to help. Let's get you somewhere safe.* She relaxes and jokes about the size of the gloves she's been handed, pleased to be the centre of attention. Their belongings are distributed between the group. The Labrador does a mad dance in the snow before he's caught and put on a lead.

They start making their way down, following in each other's deep footsteps. It's snowing sideways and the ice crystals bite into exposed cheeks like tiny daggers. The sound of the wind breaks up the radio traffic. *Starting the descent now. Going north. Approximately fifteen minutes to the vehicle. Over.* The man wishes he'd accepted a coat, or at least a hat, but is too proud to say so. He can hear his wife in front, chatting away, but can't make out what she's saying. The young man ahead of her laughs. The thick curtain of snow suddenly disappears, revealing the flashing blue lights of the mountain rescue vehicle in the distance.

A few minutes later, the couple climb into the backseat, the dog panting happily between them, his tongue flicking spittle everywhere. *What about the others?* his wife asks. They will follow on foot. The husband offers his seat, but nobody takes any notice and the heavy door slams shut.

The Land Rover starts a slow journey down the slippery track in first gear, the engine whirring in a high pitch. The fans are pumping out plumes of hot air, thawing cold fingers. The man can't feel his toes anymore and wonders if he's got frostbite. Halfway down, the road is partially blocked by a snowdrift. The team members jump out with shovels in hand, leaving the family alone in the car.

He leans over the dog to check on his wife. She is smiling at the baby, his mouth wide open in a grin, gums showing a couple of white specks of enamel. She's too preoccupied to acknowledge her husband's presence. He sits back and ruffles the wet, smelly coat of the Labrador. He checks his phone, no signal.

It's not long before the family are deposited in front of The Black Bull Inn with their belongings scattered around them. Down here, the snow has already melted; a thousand feet makes a big difference.

The husband produces a wedge of cash from the inside of his jacket. He thinks about the contract he might lose and how much it will cost him as he peels off five twenties to give to the driver. A donation for the team. He likes to think of himself as generous, but the truth is he doesn't want to be in debt to anyone. An hour's work for four people, not a bad hourly rate.

The driver feels awkward taking the money but thanks the man for his contribution. Does he think the team is a taxi firm? The man clearly isn't aware of the team members on the other side of the hill, having dug through snow drifts for an hour. Why should he worry about their partners at home finishing dinner on their own or having to cancel engagements because it's too short notice to get a babysitter? Or the cost of maintaining the vehicles and equipment? The hundred pounds is at best an insurance premium, an insurance he's paid for after he's already claimed on it. A bit of gratitude would have been enough, but the driver doesn't tell him.

The husband holds the baby while his wife hands back the coat, hat and gloves. She laughs and thanks the rescuer with a hug. When did she last laugh? He can't remember. Her face has softened, the lines around her mouth are the result of a wide smile. It strikes him how beautiful she is. There is a sparkle in her dark green eyes that he's not seen in a long time. She doesn't stare at him with hatred anymore and he feels ashamed for losing his temper. *Weren't we lucky? We could have frozen to death up there*, she says. There's no blame in her voice. Their baby boy yawns and nuzzles his head into his dad's warm neck. The dog blanket falls away and the husband takes comfort from the smell of his son's hair.

That's when it hits him, their vulnerability, the danger they were in. Who said what, or what happens tomorrow, is irrelevant. What matters is that they're safe. The mountain rescue Land Rover is about to drive off when he knocks on the driver's window. *I forgot to say thank you. I really mean it.*

He returns to his wife with a strange feeling brewing in his stomach and pressure building behind his eyes. He hugs her and the baby tight. The warm inviting light from the pub window beckons them inside. He feels lucky indeed.

Flip Flop, Flip Flop

'Look at that, Fifi!' I said, pointing to the packed car park in the middle of the village. Typical. A hot and sunny weekend draws every man, woman and dog into the great outdoors. That's when we get called out the most. Just the volume of people, I suppose. Combine that with the lack of preparation and common sense and you've got a recipe for disaster. Everyone thinks the countryside is a playground they can visit without a care in the world like it's welcoming them with open arms.

Fifi lifted an eyebrow and looked at me like she knew what I was thinking.

We walked past two couples in their twenties wearing designer sunglasses. They were busy unloading cool boxes and wicker picnic baskets from a small electric hatchback while music was blearing from a portable speaker. The two girls were dressed in shorts that barely covered their bottoms. Nice, but risky. I pictured their legs lobster red from lack of sun cream by the end of the day. The lads wore vests that showed off the countless hours they must have spent in the gym. None of them looked like they had ever encountered mud unless they'd bought it for a small fortune to apply as a facemask.

Knowing the path well, I shook my head in disbelief watching them head up Gunnerside Gill with only flimsy flip-flops on their feet. I continued down the road but my mind was full of broken ankles and dislocated toes. Convinced we'd soon have a callout, I no longer enjoyed my walk and returned home.

'Eleonor?' I called to my wife as I entered our hallway. She was in the kitchen writing a thank you letter to the Search and Rescue Dog Association that for the fifth month in a row had awarded Fifi a prize for being the most successful search dog in the country. 'The gill is filling up with people determined to injure themselves. I'm going to head out to take a look instead of waiting at home all day for a callout.'

'Whatever makes you happy,' Eleonor shouted back.

I detected ridicule in her voice and was about to bring up the fact that once I had actually discovered someone who had required the help from the rescue team, but decided against it, not wanting to reopen that can of worms.

'Leave Fifi here. I need to trim her claws this morning,' Eleonor added.

Setting off along the narrow and uneven footpath that follows the stream at the bottom of Gunnerside Gill, I felt reassured I had my mountain rescue backpack. It contains everything you'd need to get yourself or others out of trouble, including ropes, radio, first aid kit and group shelter. I doubted I'd need the spare gloves and hats but left them in anyway. You never know.

Sharp rocks and large boulders made the walk slow going. I was just beginning to wonder where the flip-floppers were when loud shrieks bounced between the sides of the narrow valley. I knew it! I turned a corner and there they were. The four of them were standing in the middle of the beck, water up to their calves, splashing it around, laughing their heads off. The cool boxes, picnic baskets and a pink blanket were scattered across a patch of grass next to the stream.

They smiled and waved at me as I walked past, staring sternly at them. Still, they have to make it back in one piece. Could be a challenge as I bet those cool boxes contained alcohol.

The path contoured the steep and wooded bank following the shape of the beck. The air smelt of Lily of the Valley and wrens were singing at the top of their lungs trying to make themselves heard over the fast-flowing water. Despite the shade, it was hot and sweat dripped down my back soaking the base of my long-sleeved shirt.

After a few minutes, I came across an old man with spindly legs sticking out of his rolled-up corduroy trousers. He was balancing on wet rocks trying to cross the beck while cradling a camera with a telescopic lens in the crook of his arm. I hid behind a tree to avoid startling him, staying close just in case he slipped. He looked so frail that the water might sweep him downstream, especially if he broke his hip landing on a rock. I held my breath as he placed his feet on various rocks, each wobblier than the next. I gasped as he lost his balance, waving his free arm in the air. But instead of falling, he plunged a foot into the cold water. Resigned to getting wet, he waded across the rest of the stream and carried on walking oblivious to my presence.

From there onwards, the woodland disappeared, revealing views of the surrounding fells. Ancient mining ruins dotted the valley and everywhere I looked small groups of people were making use of footpaths and bridleways to explore the gill. Three mountain bikers hurtled downhill crossing the footpath in front of me without a care in the world, or any helmets and knee pads for that matter. They wouldn't be so gung ho if they'd seen the injuries that I'd come across. I can promise you that!

I stopped tutting when I noticed some colourful dots on the opposite side of the valley. Through my binoculars, I identified three men scrambling up a bank covered in scree and tufts of coarse moorland grass. The gradient was steep enough that every time they moved, pebbles were dislodged, tumbling down the hill. Below them, a family with two children, a girl and a boy dressed in pastel-coloured outfits, were having a picnic oblivious to the danger lurking above. I aimed my binoculars back towards the men. They had stopped for a breather, looking out over the valley, hands resting on their hips. One man in particular was of a hefty build and despite the distance I noticed that his face was the colour of a tomato. It was going to take them a long time to climb that loose hillside before reaching the track at the top. I wondered what would come first, a heart attack, heat stroke or a head injury from falling rocks? To prevent the latter, I knew I had to act fast.

I sprinted down the slope towards the stream, waving my arms, calling out to the family. The heavy backpack caused my centre of gravity to be higher than normal and I quickly gathered pace. The father was busy attending to a disposable BBQ and the mother had her nose in a book, but luckily the little boy spotted me and pulled at his dad's t-shirt. Once I had their attention I came to a halt and motioned to them to move further downstream, shouting, 'Rocks, rocks!'

I had also attracted the attention of the three men, who assumed there was an emergency and immediately began making their way down the slope in a cascade of boulders and rocks. I watched in horror at the carnage unfolding in front of me.

The family, peppered by small pebbles and witnessing several larger stones landing at their feet, had now realised that they were in danger. The mother grabbed a child in each hand and started running, their escape route made harder by an awkward wooden gate in the drystone wall separating their field from the next. She held the gate open and her children squeezed through, followed by the husband. His fingertips were clasping the sides of the flimsy aluminium BBQ, where a dozen sausages were already burning. In my mind, the scene evolved to catastrophic proportions involving multiple casualties suffering burns in addition to head injuries from falling rocks, heart attacks and heat stroke with a few broken legs thrown in for good measure.

I started running only for the ground to come up and hit my face.

When I came around a bunch of curious face were staring down at me. To my right were a couple of the mountain bikers I'd seen earlier, to my left, the large man with the red face with his two friends towering behind him. By my feet stood the mother and father, with their children sitting cross-legged in front, eating bread rolls containing black sausages.

'Look Mummy!' said the little boy when he noticed that I had opened my eyes.

'Oh, good. Are you okay?' asked his mother, dropping to her knees.

'We saw you fall,' the red-faced man said spitting in my face as he leaned over me to make sure I'd seen him.

'Are you hurt?' asked one of the mountain bikers who looked about fifteen with a face full of pimples and faint tufts of pubescent facial hair.

I moved my legs slightly and two things dawned on me. The first was that it was unlikely I had broken my spine as the pain from moving my left leg nearly made me throw up. The second thing I realised was that I was going to endure the most humiliating event in my entire life, having to call out my own mountain rescue team to carry me off. If I had been able to crawl the two miles back to the road without anyone spotting me, I would have attempted it. But with so many people by my side, there was no way I could've slithered off unnoticed. I fished my phone out of my shirt pocket. No signal. I knew from experience that my team radios wouldn't work here either.

'I can run back to the village and phone for help,' a young voice came from somewhere above my head.

'Right, call the police and tell them it's a well-equipped hill walker with a lower leg injury and possible concussion.' I looked at my navigation app and rattled off a ten-figure grid reference.

'Sure, I'll run as fast as I can!'

My heart sank as the sound of *flip flop flip flop* faded into the distance.

The crowd stayed patiently by my side, apart from one of the mountain bikers whose offer of going to the village to check that help had been summoned I had gladly accepted.

When help finally arrived an hour and a half later, I was prepared to get ridiculed. But the rescue party consisted of only Jenny and Tom, two recently qualified team members, each carrying half of a stretcher on their backs. They had panic written across their faces and didn't even recognise who I was at first.

'This isn't much of a turnout, is it?' I asked, concerned about what the others in the group might think about such a feeble response from our rescue team.

'Sorry, everyone else has been diverted to the big job at the waterfalls in Keld,' Tom said.

I sighed. Not only was I missing what sounded like a serious rescue most likely involving lots of ropework and helicopters, as they usually did when we got called to Keld, but I was also putting an extra strain on the team.

'Are you happy to help carry the casualty?' Tom asked. I thought he'd asked me before I spotted all the nodding faces around me. Even the little girl nodded, her eyes full of excitement. Without ceremony, I was asked to drag myself onto the assembled stretcher. Jenny secured the straps across my body and tied six nylon carry straps, three on each side.

The shortest route back to the village was the route I had come, meaning a challenging stretcher carry. On my left, I had Tom and two pink-faced youths still wearing their flip-flops, both medical students it had turned out. On my right was Jenny, then the red-faced man who transpired to be a police officer, and last in line the father, who had thankfully decided to leave the BBQ behind. Everyone else was following us carrying bags and pushing bicycles. We arrived back in the village only to discover that the ambulance had been diverted to Keld. Instead, my wife was waiting in the car park, arms crossed, her head tilted sideways. She had that smug look on her face that I particularly hate, mixed with annoyance at having to come back from Keld to take me to A&E in Darlington.

Six hours later, we were at home watching TV, Fifi curled up between us on the sofa. The x-ray had failed to find any broken bones, and my pain was politely attributed to stretched ligaments and severe bruising, which apparently can be more painful than a fracture. My foot was resting on the coffee table tightly strapped into an orthopaedic boot. While Eleonor sipped a large glass of my favourite red wine, I was nursing a cup of tea as I had been told not to consume alcohol that evening, due to my mild concussion.

'Stop staring at me like that.' I snapped.
'Like what?'

'Like you think I'm an idiot. Like I deserved what happened today.'

'It served you right to be stretchered off by people in flip-flops.' Eleonor laughed and leaned back on the sofa waiting for me to take the bait. I didn't disappoint.

'Well, you should have seen them. Walking casualties, they were.'

'So how come you were the one that had to be rescued then?'

'I was just unlucky.'

'And if anything had happened to them? That wouldn't have been bad luck? Do you think they deserved to have accidents?'

'No, course not.'

'Stop being so judgy then.' Eleonor did another one of her laughs of superiority that I'm sure Cleopatra would have been proud of.

'It's not just about being unlucky. Failing to prepare is like preparing to fail.'

'So what's it going to be, were you or were you not unlucky today? What caused you to injure yourself? You had all the kit and wore all the right things, didn't you?'

I felt her questions were penning me in like a sheep for slaughter. What had caused me to fall? I thought back on the events of the day. And then I got it. The group of youths, yes, they were woefully underequipped according to my standards, but they must have concentrated on every stride while walking along that footpath to not stub their toes or twist their ankles. The old man crossing the stream hadn't even noticed me watching him as his whole attention was focused on staying on his feet. The same with the family, if I hadn't started shouting at them they might have noticed the odd pebble coming down and slowly moved away rather than the calamity that had ensued. I had become the casualty because I had wanted to police everyone else instead of paying attention to where I was putting my feet. I had no intention of admitting this to my wife and instead changed the topic.

'Thanks for taking me to the hospital, really appreciate it.'

'You're welcome.'

'Any chance you could bring me some cheese and biscuits?'

A Tiger in the Dale

Lucy hands Ray a faded photo.

'Yes, I remember it well,' he says.

It shows three men in their early thirties standing in front of what Lucy assumes is the local pub. The middle chap has a pornstar moustache, bushy sideburns and is wearing flared jeans and a shirt with a dark green ivy leaf pattern dotted with pineapples. He is holding a poster with a roaring cartoon tiger sitting on a round circus platform with 'Connie's Circus Sensation' printed in large red lettering at the top.

'That's you in the middle, isn't it?' Lucy asks. 'Next to my grandad, on the left.'

'You mean right. To the left is Jerry, bless his soul.'

'Sorry, I meant right.' She points to her grandfather Henry, a blond man dressed in an orange t-shirt. His thick-rimmed glasses look like a pair of TV screens. She feels a pang of sadness that it has been years since she saw him, and now it's too late. 'I've cleared out the last of his things this afternoon and found the photo tucked into one of his maps. It's a bit unusual, isn't it? Do you know anything about it?'

Ray nods, but his face stays motionless like it's turned into stone.

Lucy wonders if calling in to see her grandfather's best friend before heading back to Surrey has been a bad idea. Ray might have dementia and now he's been put the spot.

'The police gave us those posters so we'd know what we were looking for. Like we didn't know what a tiger looked like. Or perhaps they thought we might get it mixed up with a different one, I don't know.'

Lucy glances to where Ray's feet would have been if he'd had any.

'No, no. That wasn't the tiger. Diabetes did that.' Ray's laugh quickly turns into a rattling cough, like someone has filled his chest with empty tin cans.

They're sitting in a small garden, at the back of Ray's stone cottage. The wheels of his wheelchair have sunk into the gravel and when he tries to move, they dig in deeper. Lucy gets up to give him a push, but Ray waves to her to sit down again.

'I told 'er indoors, it was a bad idea. But at least she knows where I am now.' Ray leans over to get a view of the kitchen window and shouts, 'That pot of tea on its way yet?'

Margaret's holding a phone to her ear as she leans towards the window and smiles apologetically.

'So this was one of your callouts?' Lucy asks Ray who is still holding the photo.

'You could say that. It must have been '76, that really hot summer. You can see the team's Land Rover in the background. The clutch went soon after. It was an unreliable beast.' Ray sighs and shakes his head. 'That must have been the last photo taken of Jerry.'

Lucy looks at the thin man on the left. His hair is combed sideways and he's wearing a checked shirt. His index finger is pointing at the tiger on the poster and he's smiling at the camera. His arm is wrapped around Ray's shoulders.

They sit in silence until Ray clears his throat. 'I suppose you want to know what this was all about?'

'Only if you want to tell me.'

Ray nods and with his eyes closed begins to speak…

I was on my knees among the weeds at the bottom of the garden assembling the aluminium frame for Margaret's new greenhouse. It was a sunny Saturday in July. The nettles were particularly aggressive, and I'd already smashed a pane of glass, so was in a foul mood.

Henry popped his head over the dry-stone wall separating the two cottages and shouted, 'You'll never believe this.'

'What?' I hissed back before returning to the joint I was screwing together.

'The police just called. They're heading over from Richmond. We need to gather the rescue team.'

I stood up and stretched my back. 'What's happened?'

'A tiger, is what's happened. It's loose on the fell!' Henry grinned like a Cheshire cat. That's the kind of guy he was. Anything new and unusual and he was all over it.

Forty-five minutes later, a dozen team members had gathered outside the village hall, but there were no signs of the police and people were turning impatient.

'Someone must have played a prank on you, Henry. A tiger, here?' Jerry asked. 'How on earth could there be a tiger in Swaledale?'

'I know Sergeant Fielding. It's not a prank,' Henry replied.

It was true. Sergeant Fielding was as straight as they came.

Margaret tugged at my arm and pointed to a poster on the village noticeboard.

'Well, I'll be damned…' I said, just as the Richmond police arrived.

'So Margaret was also in the team?' Lucy asks.

'Yes, yes, we joined a year or so after the team had formed. All we did was a bit of training now and again. We didn't have many callouts in the first few years. Not many people knew we even existed, let alone how to call us out.'

'Sorry for interrupting, please continue.'

Sergeant Fielding, flanked by two of his constables, gathered us in a semi-circle.

'As you'll know by now,' Fielding gave a nod to Henry, 'we're having a problem with a missing cat.'

A few team members chuckled, drawing a disapproving glare from the sergeant.

'I suggest not using the 'T' word if at all possible to avoid worrying residents and visitors needlessly.'

'So you're saying we have a pussy problem,' Jim piped up with a cigarette bobbing up and down in the corner of his mouth. He was a slim young chap with a pockmarked face and the knack of being at the right place at the right time. No one could ever remember inviting him to join the team but, for some reason, he had already become part of the furniture.

'Yes, a rather large pussy problem,' Sergeant Fielding responded straight-faced.

'Do we need guns?' I asked, probably sounding too keen for Fielding's liking.

'No, no, we're in discussion with the gamekeepers about such matters. We would like you to comb the paths and tracks in the area and persuade any hikers you come across to return to their accommodation.'

'Have there been any sightings of the tiger?' Margaret asked.

'Shhhh...' could be heard from the other team members.

'I'm not going to use the term pussy. This is the Dale. If we know a tiger is on the loose then it's no longer a secret. I bet half the village already knows.' Margret pointed at the road. *'Look! They're already getting their sheep down.'*

Sure enough, a large number of tractors with sheep trailers were passing through the village. A couple of farmers carrying shotguns were heading for the path that led onto the fell. They weren't even stopping to eavesdrop on us which was proof enough that they already knew.

'Alright,' Sergeant Fielding said, *'let's call it a tiger then.'*

'Is it a Sumatran or a Siberian tiger?' Jerry asked. *'Or perhaps a Bengal? Male or female?'*

He was a very inquisitive young man and as a farmer's boy, he knew a lot about animals. Sergeant Fielding assumed he was taking the piss and ignored him.

At this point, a flock of ewes with their lambs in tow passed the village hall, herded by Percy Clatver and his two three-legged collies. *'I'm not letting my girls become tiger food,'* Percy shouted to the officer.

'Right, then,' Fielding said, *'let's get those walkers off the hill as soon as we can. Looks like the smorgasbord available to our tiger is becoming more limited by the minute. We'll do a debrief in the village hall at seven tonight.'*

Fielding returned to his van, followed by his constables, who hadn't said a single word but had done a great deal of nodding to everything that had been said.

Henry unfolded an Ordnance Survey map. Within a few minutes, he'd split the team into pairs and selected footpaths and tracks to be checked. I was paired with Jerry. Margaret would go with Henry.

'Did I hear my name mentioned?' Margaret says as she appears carrying a tray of tea and digestive biscuits.

'Ray's telling me about the time the tiger escaped,' says Lucy looking up at Margaret expecting a smile. But no smile is forthcoming.

Margaret's mouth is tense and sharp lines have formed above her lip. 'Oh, that old story.' She puts cups and saucers on the wrought iron garden table, then freezes like she's about to say something. Ray shuffles nervously in his wheelchair.

'I can't believe Grandad never mentioned it,' Lucy says breaking the awkward silence.

'Did he not? Well, not everyone wants to dwell on that episode.' Margaret returns inside, leaving Lucy looking at Ray for clarification. He waves his hand to brush it off. 'It was traumatic for Margaret. We haven't spoken about it much since those days. But you ought to know the story.'

'Before you carry on,' Lucy says, pouring tea into two porcelain cups, 'how come the circus had lost a tiger?'

'Apparently, Connie's circus was travelling up the dale for their next performance in Muker when the tiger wagon came off the road just before Gunnerside. Before anyone had time to react, the tiger had disappeared into Rowleth Woods.'

'I see. So what happened next?'

Jerry and I spent the afternoon clearing the paths on the hillside to the east of Gunnerside Gill. The air was clear, the sun shone bright and I both hoped and feared there would be a tiger behind every stone wall. We were following a footpath through the fields when I noticed Jerry's eyes peeled on the ground instead of taking in the views.

'What are you looking for?' I asked him.

'Paw prints, droppings. You know, tiger stuff.'

I spotted numerous piles of faeces in the grass. 'Do you know what tiger poo looks like?'

'Not really, but I know what the normal stuff looks like, so if we find something I haven't seen before, we can presume it's the tiger.'

'We aren't supposed to track down the tiger, remember? Only warn people,' I pointed out.

'I prefer to find the tiger before it finds me if that's alright with you.'

That made sense and since there weren't any walkers around, I began looking out for unusual turds.

At a muddy gap between two fields, I noticed a large paw print and my heart did a double beat. 'Hey, look at this! It's huge!' I said and grabbed Jerry's shirt sleeve.

He leant over and shook his head.

'Dog. Big dog, but not a tiger.'

'How can you be sure?'

'The claw marks. Cats pull their claws in when they walk, dogs can't.'

An hour later we reached the ruins of Blakethwaite smelt mill. It's a beautiful spot in the junction of three narrow valleys and marks the boundary of the area we'd been asked to clear. We sat down on a rock for a rest while admiring a small waterfall. I was hot and was about to suggest we should cool off in the stream when an older couple in sturdy boots, red socks and big rucksacks descended towards us on sinewy legs.

As the more senior team member, I took charge. 'Sorry to disturb your hike today. Unfortunately, there has been an incident and we strongly advise you to take the shortest route to Gunnerside.'

'What do you mean by incident?' the chap enquired while repeatedly looking at his wife to make sure she found the news as disagreeable as he did. By her stern look, it was obvious that she did.

'We have accommodation booked in Reeth so going to Gunnerside doesn't work for us,' she said with her eyebrows lowered to emphasise how much we had inconvenienced her.

'For your safety, I would recommend–' Jerry chipped in before she interrupted him.

'We're doing the coast-to-coast you see and Reeth is our next stop, not Gunnerside.'

'And anyway, who are you?' the husband asked.

In those days we didn't have mountain rescue jackets so we would have looked like a random pair of hippies.

'We are from Swaledale Fell Rescue,' I said, hoping they would take my word for it. *'The police have tasked us with clearing the fells of walkers.'*

'But why on earth would you do that? Look at the sky, not a cloud in sight,' the lady said and laughed like she was addressing an idiot. *'I've never heard anything more preposterous in my life! No doubt you'll ask for a donation next!'* The lady did inverted commas in the air. *'We're not falling for your tricks.'*

I looked at Jerry and shrugged my shoulders.

'Come on, Geoffrey. Let's move on.' The lady strode off shaking her head, followed by her husband.

I found myself wishing the tiger would appear.

'What did the Roman say when his wife was eaten by a tiger?' Jerry asked me once the couple had disappeared over the brow of the hill.

'Don't know.'

'Gladiator!' he said and laughed.

While returning to Gunnerside, we didn't meet any more walkers or see any sheep. Even the rabbits that normally plagued the hillsides were absent. Maybe the smell of the tiger had driven them inside their burrows. It was an uncomfortable thought that we might be the only tiger food for miles around.

Back in Gunnerside, a crowd had gathered outside the village hall. At first, I thought it was journalists, but when I got closer I spotted the placards. 'Save Our Tiger!', 'A Free Tiger is a Happy Tiger!' and 'No To Trophy Hunters!' An ensemble of hairy characters were pushing up their chests against a group of gamekeepers, with farmers spectating from the sidelines. Two constables were blowing their whistles while attempting to separate the combatants, but neither group seemed keen to back down.

Margaret and I approached Sergeant Fielding who was observing from a distance. 'What's going on?'

'Since you ask, Lord Lingworth announced that he will kick off the shooting season with a big game hunt tomorrow. He's invited two dozen of his cronies from down south.'

'Surely, that can't be allowed?'

Sergeant Fielding shook his head and winced as one of the gamekeepers was smacked on the head with a placard. 'That's what I said, but apparently, they've already scheduled a motion with Parliament to declare the 21st-28th July open season for tiger hunting.'

'Surprise, surprise. Some rich guy is going to have a tiger skin to put in front of his fire,' Margaret mumbled behind me.

'And the animal protesters?' I asked Fielding.

'Some nature guy on the TV said the Yorkshire Dales could do with a top predator to balance the ecosystem. Couldn't have been worse timing. Now the conservationists claim that a breeding programme should be established. Please excuse me.' Sergeant Fielding approached the throng of protesters to save one of the constables who was pinned up against the village noticeboard by a woman with two long plaits and beefy pink arms protruding from a purple tie-dyed t-shirt.

Henry came up behind me. 'Ow do? Seen owt?'

I shook my head. 'You?'

'A ewe without a head. Up at Smarber near Rowleth Woods.'

I swallowed hard and grimaced. It was the first tangible evidence that the tiger was real.

Henry continued, 'Yeah, not a pretty sight.'

We were interrupted by Percy Clatver firing his shotgun in the air with Sergeant Fielding standing next to him. Everyone knew the special relationship between the farmer and the policeman. It had started ten years ago with Fielding spotting Percy drunk at the wheel of his Land Rover in the early hours of the morning. In his eagerness to have a stern word, Fielding had run over Percy's mum's pregnant cat.

'If you won't tell, I won't tell...' Percy had said falling out of his car.

After Percy had assured Fielding he would stop at a couple of pints in the future and Fielding had promised not to run over any more cats, a mutual understanding had developed between the two men. Of course, Percy told everyone in the pub what had happened the very next evening, but having a contact in the police was more important than seeking retribution for a moggie, especially since his mum had already had many sleepless nights worrying about what to do with all the kittens.

The shot silenced the protesters.

'Please make your way inside in a calm and civilised manner so we can get this meeting started.' Sergeant Fielding waved for everyone to follow him.

The village hall was full. Journalists had claimed the front row. The gamekeepers and rescue team members lined the walls while farmers, visitors and animal rights protesters were seated in the middle. Even Lord Lingworth had made the effort to attend.

'Ladies and gentlemen,' Sergeant Fielding scanned the audience from the stage. You all know by now that early this morning a tiger escaped from Connie's circus as they approached Gunnerside. We quickly established

contact with the fell rescue team who assisted in clearing the hills of walkers. From what I've heard there have been no confirmed sightings of the animal.'

'One of my yaws had its rear legs bitten off, like. Clean off. Tail and all.' Percy Clatver shouted. *'Will there be compensation?'*

'My yaw had its front legs chewed. Very dead like. Chunks of meat taken from the neck,' another farmer announced.

'There's another one with its head missing up at Smarber,' Henry added.

'I'm sorry,' a lady with long red hair and round glasses said in a Home Counties accent, *'but what are these yaws that you're talking about?'*

'We'll deal with any compensation later. Let's move on,' Sergeant Fieling said and scanned the room until he found the face he was looking for. *'Please, Lord Lingworth, you've asked to say a few words.'*

Lord Lingworth, dressed in light-green tweed jacket and breeches, ascended the steps to the stage accompanied by his headkeeper who was carrying a shotgun under his arm. The tittle-tattle from the environmentalists in the audience soon fizzled out when the Lord's voice boomed across the hall.

'To protect livestock and residents, I have taken the initiative to call in a few experienced hunters to deal with the problem. We will not rest until this Dale is safe again.'

'How much are you charging them?' a man with a pink scarf and long blond hair called out. There were random whoops of support from the crowd.

'Yeah, some favour you are doing us,' the woman with red hair shouted.

'Save the tiger!' several protesters started chanting. Lingworth looked at Fielding for support.

Sergeant Fielding stepped onto the stage and thanked Lord Lingworth for his contribution, before addressing the room. 'I can promise that everyone on the force will use any means possible to prevent the tiger from causing any more damage.'

'Like hitting it with a car, Sergeant?' Jim piped up. There was a muted chuckle in the room.

After a couple of general announcements, people started to leave, keen to get home before it got dark. One or two muttered their disappointment at the lack of a raffle.

The next morning, I knocked on Henry's door. The volume of traffic was heavier than usual and not what you would expect at seven thirty on a Sunday. Henry came to the door dressed in a brown t-shirt and boxer shorts. Behind him I noticed Jerry, equally bleary-eyed. Henry's wife was away visiting her sister and it was clear that he was making the most of the weekend. I felt slightly miffed that I hadn't been invited.

'Seen this?' I asked, standing to one side so he could observe the passing rust buckets. The occupants

were exclusively male, between 20 and 30 years of age, all sporting impressive amounts of tattoos. The barrels of shotguns were gleaming in the partially wound-down car windows.

'Doesn't look like the woolly peace-loving creatures from yesterday, does it?' I said.

'And they certainly don't look like Lord Lingworth's mates from London either,' Henry muttered.

'Bunch of have-a-go hunters wanting to grab themselves a trophy tiger?' I suggested.

Henry nodded and waved for me to go through to the kitchen.

I joined Henry and Jerry for a second breakfast of toast and jam, trying to avoid the crumbs in the butter and the buttery streaks left in the jar of homemade gooseberry preserve.

'Jerry has an idea,' Henry said with his mouth full handing me a cup of tea.

I looked at Jerry.

'Well, just a thought really.'

'He wonders if the tiger suit is still in the village hall attic?' Henry asked.

'I suppose so,' I replied.

'It would be nice to try and catch the tiger alive before someone takes a pop at it,' Jerry said and wiped the crumbs from the toast from his mouth with the back of his hand.

'We'd better be quick,' I said, *'because looking at the number of guns present in the Dale today, I'd be surprised if the tiger lasted until lunchtime.'*

Jerry's plan was simple. He would dress up as a tiger cub to attract the interest of the circus tiger. If it was male it would likely want to kill him, so to prevent that from happening we'd set him up next to one of the sinkholes above Rowleth Woods. It would serve as a bear pit without the sharp spikes at the bottom. The hole was shallow enough to prevent the tiger from hurting itself, but deep enough to avoid it escaping.

'Couldn't we just tie a sheep next to the hole?' I asked.

Jerry shook his head. 'Trust me, we're not dealing with a hungry tiger judging by how many farmers claimed to have lost ewes to it.'

'Well...' I started but was interrupted by Henry.

'I like the plan, but we'd better be quick. Margaret has got the key to the hall, hasn't she?' Henry had barely finished the sentence before he had Margaret on the phone. She agreed to nip over and get it straight away.

As soon as Henry put the phone down, it rang again. This time it was Sergeant Fielding who had a lot to say for himself before Henry managed to interrupt him. 'No Sir, don't think we need to...'

The Sergeant carried on for another minute or two.

'It's not the tiger that I'm worried about, it's the army of trigger-happy gun-wielding people that concerns me. ...sure, sure. OK, let's have a briefing at four o'clock this afternoon.' Henry finished the call and looked at me and Jerry with a smile. We stared back at him, our eyebrows raised.

'We've got time to sort this out now. Let's go,' Henry said and finished his milky tea.

The stripy costume fitted Jerry perfectly. From a distance, he looked like a real tiger, especially since our brains had been determined to see one for the last twenty-four hours.

'OK, guys,' Henry addressed us as we stood next to a hole on the grassy bank above Rowleth Woods. 'The plan is as follows: Jerry, stand next to the hole and look as tigery as you can. I'm sorry about the mouldy smell. Hopefully, the real tiger isn't put off by the smell of village hall attics.'

Jerry crouched on all fours, while we gave him instructions on how to position his head and back to make him more tiger-shaped.

'That's it!' Henry shouted. 'When the tiger comes up from the woods it will fall into the hole the moment before it attacks you. Simple!' Henry turned his attention to Margaret.

'You've got the gun ready?'

Margaret nodded and picked it up off the grass.

'You hide there,' Henry pointed to a large boulder only ten metres or so from the hole. 'If it looks like the tiger is going to put your lives in danger, shoot it. But remember, the goal is to capture it alive. In the meantime, Ray and I will go in from opposite sides of the woods and drive it towards this spot.'

'How can you be so sure it's in the woods?' Margaret asked.

'Look around you. It must be hiding somewhere and this is the only place with dense enough vegetation to hide a tiger.'

Henry had a point.

At nine o'clock, I was to come in from the west while Henry would start from the east side of the woods. We counted on the tiger moving uphill to avoid us, rather than back towards the road from where it had come.

I waited by the edge of the woods, eyes peeled on the sprawling shrubs and sea of brambles that obscured the view of the forest behind. The tiger might be less than ten meters away and I wouldn't be able to spot it. Now and again I glanced at my watch. It was the longest ten minutes of my life.

In the distance, a trail of hunters were heading up the footpath into Gunnerside Gill where Jerry and I had combed the fields the previous day. On the opposite side of the valley, a few shiny Land Rovers, some of Lord Lingworth's guests no doubt, were revving hard to *navigate the rough tracks to get up on the moor. Everywhere I looked I could see people carrying guns ready to kill. I would also have liked a gun but accepted that since we only had one, Margaret was the best person to be in charge of it. She was, after Jerry, the most likely person to come into close contact with the tiger.*

I entered the woods at nine o'clock precisely holding my arms out wide calling, 'Pussy, pussy! Off you go, pussy!' I'm not sure if there's a special technique for driving tigers but that's what seemed appropriate at the time. As agreed, I moved diagonally uphill hoping to leave a gap at the top of the woods of around a hundred yards between me and Henry, enough for the tiger to spot Jerry as it left the woods, but not so narrow that it would be tempted to sneak out sideways, or God forbid attack us.

The woods were quiet except for a few startled birds. I was close to the top, thinking it had been a wasted mission, when I heard a shot followed by a second one. I forgot about being careful and ran through the woods until I reached the sinkhole where we'd left Jerry and Margaret.

Lucy waits for Ray to continue. His head is bent down and his eyes are closed. It is only when he looks up that she notices his tears.

'Well, you can guess it can't you?'

'Did the tiger kill Jerry?' she asks and reaches out for Ray's hand.

'Worse than that,' Ray says and shakes his head. 'Jerry was lying on the ground bleeding heavily from a gunshot wound to his stomach. Margaret was kneeling next to him tying her jumper tight around his middle to try and stop the blood pouring out.' Ray sighs. 'I remember it like it was yesterday. Her hands were bright red and her eyes wild with fear. She pointed up the slope towards the track that leads towards Low Row shouting, "The bastards shot him!" Henry appeared a few seconds later.'

'Gosh, that's so sad. Did they catch the shooter?'

'Of course not. So many guns on that hillside, but everyone kept quiet. Margaret's description of the vehicle kept changing so I suspect she only heard it, rather than caught sight of it. In the end, it was labelled as an accident and we heard nothing more of it.'

'But the tiger? Did you find it?'

Ray pauses and looks at the kitchen door before he turns back to Lucy. He takes a deep breath and slaps his palms on his thighs.

'No. There weren't even any sightings of it. The circus moved on. Some say they got a hefty insurance payment. Others claimed they hadn't even seen the tiger in the circus performance in Richmond the night before its alleged disappearance. Eventually, the farmers let their sheep back on the fell and things went back to normal. Rumour has it that you can see faint stripes on the sheep up above Keld when the sun hits them right.' Ray winks at her. 'Oh, and I bet you didn't know that there's still an official hunting season for tigers in the UK for the last week in July.'

Lucy looks at her watch and puts her tea cup down on the saucer. 'I'm so sorry, but I'm going to have to make a move. Got a long drive ahead. Any chance I could use the bathroom?'

'Of course. In the hallway, take the second door on the left.' Ray hands the photo back to her. 'It's been lovely to see you.'

Margaret is no longer in the kitchen so Lucy continues into the hallway in search of the bathroom. Left, right, she never is sure which is which. She opens a door to find out. It's not a bathroom, she can tell that straight away. Before she closes the door something catches her eye. Black stripes on glossy orange fur, a grinning mouth full of white pointy teeth. The skin of a tiger covers the floor between the sofa and the fireplace, the head resting on the hearth like it's about to take a chunk out of a log next to the wood-burning stove.

'Doesn't it look nice there?'

Lucy spins around to see Margaret behind her.

'It was Jerry's own fault, you know,' Margaret continues. 'If he hadn't stood up to try and stop me from shooting it, the bullet wouldn't have hit him. So naive of him to think that tiger would ever make it off that hillside alive. To what? A life in a cage? I was lucky it fell into the sinkhole after the second shot. Henry and Ray retrieved it for me the following night.' Margaret puts her finger up to her lips. 'Not a word to anyone, understand?'

Lucy nods and leaves. She doesn't stop for a wee until she finds a motorway service station.

Off the Cliff

Zoe's cheek is pressed against cold stone. The sound of rushing water fills her ears. She tries to lift her neck but it's like a rusty saw is trying to sever her head from her spine.

Oh my God, oh my God. Are you okay? Can you hear me?

It's a woman with a Scottish accent. Her purple suede boots clash with the muted autumn foliage. The woman bends down and tilts her head. She's so close that Zoe can smell her perfume and the stale cigarette smoke on her breath.

Did you fall? Oh my God. I'll get some help. Don't move.

Did she fall? Zoe can't remember. She's not even sure where she is. Trying to free her arm, she suspects something is broken. She waits, her face resting on the ground, the rest of her body in a jumbled pile that she dare not move. Deep from within is a thumping pain growing in intensity. She assumes the woman has left because she can no longer smell the perfume.

Zoe comes around again and hears voices, both male and female.

Hello, can you hear me?
Is she dead?
No, no… What's your name?
Someone puts their hand on her back.
Don't worry sweetheart. The ambulance is coming.

Zoe feels something soft being draped across her body. It smells of sour sweat but quickly makes her feel warmer. She remembers now. The waterfalls. Walking along the narrow path with Jack. Moments before… The thought evaporates as she's overwhelmed by pain.

More and more people gather, talking quietly. Someone is holding her hand. They keep asking her questions but she is only able to grunt in response. Time drags.

Beeps and crackly voices from radios break the calm. A man gets on his knees beside her, all she can see is the crotch of his green trousers until he bends down bringing his bearded face into view. His lips move but the words reach her brain all jumbled up due to the unbearable pain.

They prod and squeeze her limbs and torso. And questions, endless questions. *What's your name? Does this hurt?* She is only vaguely aware of what is going on. They turn her over, her body secured between many hands, her head held straight in line with her spine. She's wrapped in a silver foil blanket.

Turkey ready for the oven, someone says, triggering a round of laughter. Zoe doesn't get the joke.

She is placed on a vacuum mattress. *It will make it less painful during the evacuation,* they tell her before pumping the air out. It doesn't take long before the sides are stiff and Zoe can't move a single muscle.

She looks up at the blue sky. The wind dislodges a handful of yellow leaves from the trees that cover the steep river bank. To her left is a rock face. She remembers standing on the top looking down at the waterfalls and the slabs below. That must be where she is now, on those slabs. Towering above her are people dressed in red jackets and helmets. All of a sudden, their attention is caught by something else. One after the other they move away. People shout. Soon only one person remains in view. Where are they all going? Their quick abandonment stirs up panic inside her.

There's another one here. Badly smashed up.

The woman standing next to her bends down.

Did you come here with someone?

She had visited the cafe with Jack. Cheese toasties, that's what they ordered. And two teas. Then they went down to look at the waterfalls. She insisted they'd take the shortcut down the bank. She wants to tell the woman about Jack but her voice is drowned out by the roaring sound of a helicopter. Its yellow belly passes over her to come to a hover just out of her view. It's deafening. The vibrations travel through her chest.

A couple of minutes later the sound of the helicopter fades away. The noise level drops and she overhears the rescuers talking between themselves.

We'll haul her up to the path. Are they going to wait in the field? Any others coming? We need another stretcher. Can someone inform the police?

Her stomach shudders the moment she is lifted off the ground. A young man with warm dark eyes and ruddy cheeks stays with her, strapped to the side of the stretcher. Even though she hasn't said a word, he keeps talking. Warns her when the stretcher might shake, and how far it is left until the top. They reach the path and rescuers gather on either side. She's again asked questions. *Are you in pain? Feeling dizzy?* All she can think about is Jack. Why do they need to call the police?

They remove the ropes and attach nylon straps to the sides. With three people on either side, they carry her through the woods along the steep and rocky path.

The swaying motion makes her drift off into fragmented thoughts. She recalls tripping over a rock, and Jack laughing. That belittling laugh she hates. The type of laugh that only bullies use. She pushed him. He lost his balance since his hands had been tucked in the waist of his grey tracksuit bottoms. *Cow*, he shouted. Never could deal with anyone standing up to him. She pushed him again. Harder. His arms flailed in the air, trying to move away from the edge. He looked ridiculous. She couldn't help but laugh. *Moooo!* she had shouted. He'd grabbed onto the sleeve of her hoodie tied around her waist.

They emerge from the wooded slope into an open space. The bright light makes her squint. On the count of three, they put the stretcher down for a minute's rest. She can smell cow pats and grass.

Jack? She asks but her voice is raspy and weak.

The young man with the red cheeks crouches down. *What did you say?*

Is Jack okay?

He doesn't answer.

An air ambulance medic comes over, dressed entirely in fluorescent orange clothing. He gives her a couple of glances while he receives a quiet briefing, too quiet for Zoe to hear. He bends down and greets her, his face round and smiley. She can see his nose hairs.

What's your name, love?

Zoe.

Not your best day, is it?

A radio crackles into life.

Cas site from control. We're sending the police down to give you permission to recover the body. Over.

For a few seconds, there's an awkward silence. They know she's heard the message.

Zoe can neither shake nor nod as her head is firmly secured to prevent any movement of her spine.

But inside her relief is spreading from the centre of her chest to every corner of her body.

You took one hell of a tumble. What happened?

She takes her time before she answers. *Jack pushed me off the cliff.*

The Descent of Pot Noodle

Saturday started very well indeed, blue sky, sunshine, hearing the first cuckoo of the year. When my wife mentioned 'barbecue', the wind didn't pick up and no storm clouds appeared. I was sent mid-morning to purchase burgers and sausages from the supermarket, hoping to sneak in a few bottles of beer for my secret stash in the garage.

Passing our mountain rescue base, a tired-looking 1960s building that had once been a petrol station, I spotted Keith on the old forecourt. Next to him was a 10-foot-high heap of soapy foam. By the time I realised that one of our Land Rovers was hidden inside the mound of bubbles, Keith had already spotted me. He smiled and waved, forcing me to pull over.

'Craig! Doing anything this morning?'

I knew what was coming. I'd been the Equipment Officer too. Only single people or those in marriages that thrived on 'time spent apart' had ever managed more than one year in the role. Keith was in his third year and no one had dared to ask about his marital status.

The excessive foaming of the team vehicle had been deliberate to catch passing team members and I could only bow my head in respect for Keith's ingenuity.

'Do you need help with anything?' I asked, pretending I'd not been a victim of his clever entrapment. He didn't have time to reply as both our phones went off in unison. It could only be one thing, a callout. The text message said: *Cavers overdue from trip to Pot Noodle?? Contact Linda on 07700 900789.*

I hadn't read to the end before my colon convulsed with fear. I'd never been underground. Ever. For six years, I'd successfully managed to time my holidays to avoid the team's underground training and been conveniently tied up whenever we'd been called to an underground rescue. However, getting this message in the company of Keith, having just admitted I had time to spare, made not attending impossible.

'Let's make sure the underground people in the team have been notified. They don't want to miss this one,' I said to give the illusion I was both diligent and selfless.

Keith and I went inside. The wall-mounted response screen showed the availability of our team members as their replies trickled in. One after the other, they appeared red meaning unavailable. Colin - 'Bad case of halitosis', Sarah - 'Unexpectedly received a peacock in the post', Gary - 'Sorry guys, just booked a cruise to Tallinn with immediate departure, hope it goes well'. Neil - 'Available but on the north coast of Scotland, ETA 7pm'. Only young Tom had responded that he was free, requesting a lift from Grinton village since he doesn't drive. The names we hoped for didn't appear: Derek - Underground Leader, Agnes - Assistant Underground Leader, Simon, Jim and Tony. None of the cavers in the team had responded with their availability.

'Are you thinking what I'm thinking?' Keith asked me.

'Typical, isn't it? They're all underground when something like this happens. Shall we hold fire until one of them resurfaces?' I suggested.

Keith gave me a funny look. 'I'll run control. I'll also contact the police and call this Linda person.' He handed me the green folder containing a record of all known caves on our patch and said, 'Can you choose an appropriate rendezvous location?'

I ran my finger along the index of caves, hoping that it wasn't on our patch so we could pass the incident to a neighbouring team. *Abyss of Certain Death, Cavern of Eternal Darkness, Marmite Pot, Smoke Pot, Squeeze-me-tight Pot, Dangling-Death-Of-Doom Pot, Canoodle Pot, Crackpot Cave, Pol Pot, Nightmare Cavern.* No Pot Noodle.

'It's as bad as I thought,' Keith announced. 'They're trapped.'

'What do you mean?'

'All our cavers are down there. Linda, Simon's mum, told me she didn't get a lift to the opticians this morning and remembers him saying something about going down a Pot Noodle yesterday afternoon.'

I held up the folder and shook my head. 'No Pot Noodle as far as I can see.'

Keith double-checked the list.

'Canoodle Pot. That must be it.' He wrote down the grid references for the cave and a rendezvous point on the road closest to the entrance, before asking me to notify the team. 'Oh, and don't forget the extended cavers.'

I rattled off a text message to every member stating the details we had so far. Once people knew some of our own team members were trapped in Canoodle Pot, a sufficient number might beat their claustrophobia and make themselves available. I sent the same message to the group labelled 'Extended Cavers', people who at some point had volunteered to help the team in case of an underground rescue. I had no idea how many of them there were, just prayed that enough of them had their phones switched on.

The smell of rotting rubber and mouldy ropes hit me as I joined Keith in the garage. He'd opened the door to the 'underground' store, a small room full of shelves that contained all the team's cave rescue equipment. He handed me a black plastic crate containing what looked like finds from an archaeological dig, lumpy shapes coated with dried mud.

'What's this?' I asked.

'Haven't got a clue. Doesn't fall under my jurisdiction. But it's on the shelf marked '1' so stick it in the Land Rover.'

Keith followed me with a box of equally strange equipment.

I cast a glance at the monitor. The screen was scrolling so fast with green responses I couldn't read any of the names. With no time to investigate, I put it down to a software glitch.

Keith drove and I sat in the passenger seat with a map of Canoodle Pot in my lap. It looked nothing like a cave, more like the intestines of a badger. Risking motion sickness, I read the description of it out loud: 'This cave is three miles long, has many narrow passages with a few large chambers and is prone to flooding. It is unusual for this area as it has a vertical pitch of thirty metres roughly half a kilometre from the entrance.'

At the bottom someone had added in scrawly handwriting: *If we need to rescue someone from here, we're fucked!*

I felt nauseous.

The road to Canoodle Pot was narrow, and we were frequently held up by old drivers, snailing along, without a care in the world. Some even refused to let us pass even though we had our blue lights flashing. The journey felt desperately slow. About a mile from the rendezvous point, we were stuck bumper to bumper in a slow-moving procession of cars.

'What on earth is going on?' I asked craning my neck to get a view of the traffic ahead. 'What are all these people doing here? We're in the middle of nowhere.'

On either side of the track were endless hills covered in a patchwork of different shades of greeny-brown. Sections of the heather that the gamekeepers had burnt in the previous year had pale twigs contrasting with the blackened ground. There were no garden centres, no cafes, and no pretty, little waterfalls with nature trails. Not even any buildings as far as the eye could see.

In front of us, car after car pulled off the road at our RV location. Bearded men with fluffy grey hair, wearing moth-holed clothes from the seventies and eighties, emerged from their cars. I looked at Keith to see if he had an explanation. He just smiled in response.

Keith managed to thread the Land Rover between a silver-blue Vauxhall Corsa and a red Reliant Robin. I checked my phone for any messages, hoping that the underground group might have been in touch. They hadn't. Instead, I found a message from my wife saying she'd invited her mother and sister to the barbecue so I needed to add gluten-free sausages to the shopping list.

There was also a message from Tom, asking if we could pick him up on the way. I cursed as I remembered the blond mop of the youth waving at us when we passed Grinton. I'd waved back and smiled instead of stopping. We had no mobile signal so there was no way I could send a message of apology.

A man with an impressive beard and very large hands greeted us as we got out of our vehicle. His yellow and grey teeth crowded his mouth like uneven tombstones.

'Sid. Pleased to meet you! Extended cavers reporting for duty. What would you like us to do?'

His firm handshake, and the fact that halitosis hadn't prevented him from attending, made a good impression on me.

Keith showed him the map and the boxes of underground equipment we'd brought.

Sid shook his head and sucked air between his large teeth. 'We need more than that, lads. We're dealing with Canoodle Pot here. Head back and bring the boxes on shelves two and three as well. We'll need more ropes and ladders.'

'I'll go,' I said. Not only could I pick up Tom along the way and message my wife to let her know I'd been called out, but most importantly, it would put off me entering the cave by at least an hour or two.

'Yeah, that'd be good. We'll get things up and running while you're away,' Keith handed me the keys to the Land Rover.

Both Sid and Keith seemed able to handle the situation. The same could not have been said about some of the people who were now making their way up the road. An army of mostly old men was heading my way, reminding me of a scene from a zombie film. Some had large bellies protruding through the centre of their muddy and scuffed caving suits that hadn't been worn in decades and therefore shrunk at least two sizes. Perhaps there were women and youths present, but dressed in similarly filthy overalls and helmets, they were impossible to distinguish from the rest. I wondered if we had a process for removing extended cavers from the team, but judging from the evidence in front of me I already knew the answer.

I even had to weave the Land Rover around an old chap in a wheelchair being pushed up the hill by what I presumed was his wife. Not far behind them was a man with a white stick and dark glasses, getting dragged along by a border collie with its long pink tongue hanging out of its mouth. I tutted and shook my head in disbelief, happy to leave Sid and Keith in charge.

Halfway to the depot, my phone picked up the messages that had been waiting for me. I pulled up to check if any were urgent. Neil had messaged saying his ETA now was 8 pm, as he'd had a puncture. Tom sent a message wondering if I was coming back later for him or if he should ask his mum for a lift. I rattled off a message saying I'd let him know when I was returning from the depot so he could wait by the road again.

At the base, I went into the store with the underground equipment and located shelves two and three. They held more crates, but also half a dozen yellow caving bags. I peeked inside some of them and was pleased to see lengths of grey rope and coiled-up wire ladders. I hurled them all into the backseat of the car and set off back up the valley. I only realised after I'd lost mobile signal that I'd forgotten to message my wife or Tom before I'd left the depot.

Back at the RV, I spotted Keith and Sid standing next to a coffee van with steaming cups. On their left was a large blue truck providing roast pork sandwiches from a pig on a rotating spit. On the other side was an ice cream van. There were still cavers arriving, most joining the queue at the catering vans to stock up on calories before trudging up the hill.

'How civilised!' I said, slamming the Land Rover door behind me.

'No point waiting until everyone's hungry before calling in the welfare units,' Sid said. 'What can I get you?'

'Coffee, please, just milk, no sugar.'

He waved at the large-breasted lady with bright orange hair who was managing the van and bypassed the dozen or so cavers that were waiting in the queue.

'Nobody told me underground callouts had catering,' I said to Keith. 'Why doesn't anyone from the team apart from the cavers want to attend them if they're this good?'

'Just another well-kept secret,' Keith replied and winked at me.

I got a feeling that there was something he wasn't telling me. It all seemed too laid back and unprofessional. Where was the urgency and the police with flashing blue lights? Surely some worried relatives would have turned up by now. 'What did you say to the guy in the wheelchair? A bit optimistic, turning up to a rescue…' I whispered to Keith.

'Oh, you mean Brian! We sent him in first,' he replied.

I scrunched my eyebrows together. 'Surely, you're joking?'

'He assured us that there's hardly anywhere in the entire cave system where it's even possible to stand up, so no need for legs. Turns out he's the one who drew the map of Canoodle Pot, so he'd know! All that was needed was a strong pair of arms, so his wife went down with him.'

'But the blind guy?'

'He went in as well. His dog knows this cave, hates it with a vengeance, and has learned to find his way out even in the dark. If the torches stop working, Vaughan and Buster will be great assets down there.'

Sid returned with my coffee in one of his giant hands. After finishing our drinks we grabbed as much equipment as we could carry across the two hundred metres of steep, lumpy moorland that separated the cave from the road.

An old lady wearing strong glasses was sitting in a camping chair next to the entrance. She had filthy brown hands and was busy filling in sheets of paper attached to a red clipboard.

'Mavis is doing the gatekeeping and records anyone and anything that enters the hole,' Sid explained.

Mavis pushed her glasses to the top of her head and gave me a muddy handshake. I fought the desire to rub my hand clean on the grass and discreetly wiped it on the back of my jacket.

'How many are down there?' Keith asked.

Mavis flicked through several sheets and counted quietly to herself. 'Ninety-four. Ninety-five if this guy goes down.' She pointed at me.

I shook my head. 'I've brought a bag of rope but I'm happy to let someone else take it in.'

A man with a large bushy moustache came up from behind and took the bag from me.

'Jeremy Shufflebottom,' he told Mavis and glanced at the side of the bag. '100 metre rope.'

Mavis recorded him on the sheet and gestured for him to enter.

The caver got on his hands and knees in front of the small triangle-shaped hole between two stone blocks that was the opening to Canoodle Pot. He leaned forward to dive in head first when a black and white blur shot out of the hole. By sheer luck, the muddy dog ran straight into my arms. I kept a firm hold of his collar.

'Ah, Buster! I'd better tick you off the list.' Mavis flicked several sheets over, found his entry, and wrote down his exit time.

'Oh look,' I said and loosened a sheet of dirty paper that had been tied around Buster's collar. It said: *Send in the following: 1 Buster, 2 Ropes, 3 Wire Ladders, 4 Hot drinks (tea if available, milk and sugar)*. On the back of the note someone had scribbled: *Bring everything from shelves 9 and 10.* I held the note up for everyone to see.

'I'd better go and get another rope and three wire ladders then,' Sid muttered. 'Will you gentlemen help me carry the four teas from the catering van?'

I glanced at Keith to see if he still felt Sid was competent to lead the rescue, but he refused to meet my gaze and instead followed. A stream of people in muddy suits and helmets was still heading for the cave entrance as I made my way back down to the cars.

'Would you mind going back for the stuff on shelves 9 and 10?' Keith asked me when I caught up with him at the Land Rover.

'I thought we only had six shelves in the underground store?' It was another reminder that avoiding underground training sessions had left big gaps in my knowledge.

'Shelves 7 to 10 are in the underground store of the underground store,' Keith said and grinned at me.

'What? There's an underground store inside the underground store?'

'They claimed they needed more space. Personally, I think they just fancied doing some digging. Anyway, you might as well bring some spare suits and helmets too.'

I drove off wondering if the world around me was going mad. In the same place as before, where the road runs close to the river, messages poured into my phone. An update from Neil:

So sorry, road closure, ETA 9 pm.

Another message from Tom:

Have you set off yet?

I texted back: *Meet me at the depot in half an hour.* A message from my wife:

Where are you? When will you be back? Mum's already here.

Instead of rattling something off, I decided to think carefully about the reply to my wife's message and then immediately forgot all about it.

Back at the base, I found the trap door to the underground store inside the underground store and used all my strength to lift it open. Feeling slightly claustrophobic, I climbed down the ladder to find a room half the size of the one above. Shelf 7 was empty and I suspected that whatever had been stored there might now be found in Canoodle Pot. Shelf 8 contained shiny new kit - carabiners, descenders, ascenders and clean white rope. There were heaps of spades and pickaxes, still with the paper stickers attached. Red and blue caving suits in their plastic packaging were stacked dozens deep next to glossy helmets. I stashed a few suits and helmets into a bin bag and moved on to shelves 9 and 10. To my surprise, these held barrels of beer, bottles of rum, and enough snacks to last a nuclear winter. Could they have mixed up the shelf numbers?

My ponderings were interrupted by a loud bang from the hatch slamming shut above my head. I tried to push it open, but it wouldn't budge. I banged on the hatch as hard as I could, while panic was building inside my chest. At least I wouldn't go hungry or thirsty. I was about to re-evaluate the situation in a more positive way when Tom's face appeared above me as he opened the hatch from the outside.

We arrived at Canoodle Pot half an hour later with the contents of shelves 9 and 10 plus the spare suits and helmets. With as much as we could carry, Tom and I trudged up to the cave.

'Oooo, they will be pleased you've brought more supplies,' Mavis said as we stacked the alcoholic drinks and salty snacks next to the entrance, Sid and Keith nodding approvingly.

'How's it going?' I asked.

'Not much to report, I'm afraid. Buster hasn't been back, which is worrying.' Sid looked at Mavis. 'When did the last guy go in?'

'Over forty minutes ago. Terry Jonason.'

'And before him?'

'Billy Broads.'

Sid's face stiffened as he drew air between his teeth once again.

As if on cue the dirty face of a middle-aged man with a monobrow appeared in the hole.

'We can't get past Big Billy Boy. He's wedged solid in the Cheese Press.'

I looked at Keith and then at Sid.

'Not the Cheese Press,' Sid sighed. 'It's the tightest passage before the pitch. I told Billy he shouldn't go down, but he insisted. Said he'd only have to breathe in a bit. I'll be right back.'

We watched Sid walk down to the catering vans, where he conversed with the man in the roast pork truck.

I assumed he needed some food or coffee to help him work out a plan for how to proceed. After a couple of minutes, the man handed Sid two plastic containers of cooking oil.

'This should get things moving,' Sid told us when he returned. 'Due to the seriousness of the situation and now having... how many, Mavis?'

'Two hundred and sixty-eight.'

'Two hundred and sixty-eight cavers trapped underground. It's probably best if I go in myself to help free Billy Boy. This boy here,' Sid handed a container to Tom, 'can help me carry some oil. We'll take some more food and drink down too.' He glanced at the large pile of boxes and 5-litre beer kegs stacked by the entrance. 'That was on shelves 9 and 10?'

'Yes, half of it is still down there,' I replied and pointed down the hill, wondering if salty snacks and rum were what the cavers were expecting.

'I'll give you a hand with it Sid,' Keith said and then winked at me and said, 'Unless you fancy it Craig?'

'Please go ahead,' I replied, 'I'll bring up the rest from the car.'

Keith and Tom put on new caving suits and helmets and soon everyone had slithered into the dark opening. Mavis assisted by threading a small beer keg through the entrance to Keith's eager hands inside, followed by a box of salty snacks for Terry to carry.

By the time they had all disappeared underground, the wind had picked up and dark storm clouds drifted in from the west. I checked my phone while returning to the vehicle. My wife had sent me seventeen new messages, the last one an emoji of a raised middle finger.

It was now coming up to eight o'clock. We had gone from five trapped cavers to well over two hundred. Things were not looking good. The catering vans had all gone. All that remained were abandoned cars, with nobody around for miles. I looked up towards the entrance but couldn't even see the light from Mavis's head torch anymore. There was only a sliver of pale sky over the hills that would soon disappear, leaving the valley in total darkness.

Laden with another keg of beer and a box of rum, with legs aching and arms feeling like they wouldn't look out of place on an orangutan, I climbed back up the hill only to find that Mavis had disappeared too.

Now here I am, sitting next to the entrance, getting drenched by torrential rain. Everything about this rescue seems wholly inappropriate. It feels like a bad dream, conjured up from guilt from not attending any underground practice sessions. I finally accept that I too will have to go down the dark passage.

Dressed in one of the caving suits, with a box of rum under my arm, I manage to slide inside the hole and begin to crawl across the wet and muddy boulders, deeper and deeper into the hillside. The air is damp and smells of farts from the two hundred cavers that have come before me. The passage twists and turns with large rocks partially blocking my progress. I find my arms and legs in positions I never thought possible, while discovering muscles I've never needed to use before. I cursed the fact that I hadn't had a piss before entering.

The scraping of my caving suit on the gritty rock drowns any other sounds out. I stop frequently, disappointed to only hear dripping water and the rumbling of a stream in the far distance. I feel truly alone.

After an eternity of slithering through narrow passages, my route looks blocked by rocks, some of which have a glossy coating of oil. Must be the Cheese Press. To one side of the boulder choke, there's a narrow opening and I snake my way through, confident that my rake-like, weedy stature for once is the ideal body shape. I pop out on the other side covered in muddy cooking oil, smelling of pork crackling and something else; something far less pleasant. It takes a while before my nose connects with my brain - dog turd! Damn Buster! I begin to view the muddy deposits that cover every surface with suspicion.

A couple of metres further along I reach the pitch, a metre-wide hole going straight down. To one side someone's bolted a wire ladder, its gleaming metal rungs disappearing into the dark depths below.

I stop for a rest. I'm not sure my arms or legs have enough strength left to hold on to the delicate rungs for any length of time. I'm confused. How can a day that had started so well end up in such a clusterfuck? And how come I'm the only one who seems to have noticed? That's when I hear faint thumping. It's not my heart, the rhythm is too slow and a trumpet breaks through at regular intervals. Worried that I've come down with delirium tremens, I pull out a bottle of rum from the soggy cardboard box and take a couple of deep gulps. I startle when Neil comes up behind me and I spray the front of my suit with alcohol in a coughing fit.

'Hey Craig! Fancy meeting you here. Haven't seen you underground before.' He's kitted out in full caving paraphernalia, looking as excited as a Labrador about to tuck into a burger. His left hand is wrapped around a bottle covered in bubble wrap. 'You've brought the rum! Good lad!' he continued. 'Thought I'd better bring some whisky. When did you figure it out?' he asked with a big grin on his face.

I look at him, a hundred thoughts forming in my mind at the same time. 'Figure what out?'

'The party? We always get a few of the surface guys falling for it every year.'

It all starts to make sense. The lack of police presence. The ridiculous excuses most team members had given for not attending. My vacant stare and lack of response has given away my ignorance. Neil starts to laugh.

'You poor sod. You didn't know? Oh my God. Well, you're here now. The others are in a chamber fifty metres along the passage at the bottom.'

'They've all come for a party?'

'Sure. The team's cavers go down the night before to put up lights and carry supplies in. The next day an invite goes out in the form of a spoof rescue message. It's a great fundraiser for the team, and pays for all the underground rescue kit.'

'But the message was real!' I get my phone out and hold it up for Neil to see.

'It doesn't say "North Yorkshire Police" does it? The NYP stands for North Yorkshire Potholers.'

It explains why Keith insisted on running control, so he could make sure the police weren't involved and why he was so keen to get down the cave and leave me on the surface to do all the logistics. I scroll down and see a similar message received at the same time last year, and the year before, to which I had replied unavailable without as much as a thought as to whether they'd been real or not.

'It's also a training session for the extended cavers. To check that they are still able to find their caving kit, leave their homes and remember to call in the catering,' Neil continues.

'You mean you actually have catering on real callouts?'

'Of course. They can go on for days. Don't you ever read the news?'

I think about some of the high-profile cave rescues that have been featured in the media and shudder when I realise that our team could be in charge of one of those. Perhaps I will attend some of the training sessions in the future, just in case. 'Apparently, including us, there are 275 people down here.' I say, not sure if I'm trying to impress him or raise a health and safety concern.

'That's excellent. As long as we're all out before the morning. That rain's really quite heavy and will flood the lower levels, for sure. Come on, let's join the party.' Neil waves for me to swap places so he can grab hold of the wire ladder, having first shoved his bottle inside his caving suit. 'Pass me the rum.'

I lean back, grab the box and sit up, my helmet clipping a rock that's hanging from the ceiling. A scraping sound precedes a rumble that is followed by an almighty crash. Behind my back, several tonnes of rock have come down blocking the passage to the surface. I grimace to show how sorry I am. 'What do we do now?'

Neil shakes his head, closes his eyes and says, 'Now we're fucked.'

Finding Funds

Sharon opened the door to face Gordon in the gloomy evening light. He shook his head, dropped his shoulders and sighed. 'I've got some bad news.'

Howard, the team's treasurer, cowered behind him, trying to make himself invisible.

'What's happened? Has someone died?' she asked, standing aside to let her visitors cram themselves into the small hallway of her cosy cottage, knocking over cross-country skis and poles that were leaning against the wall even though the snow had melted weeks ago.

'No, not as bad as that,' Gordon said. He bent over to gather up the ski equipment from the floor trying his best not to poke someone's eye out.

'Oh, not another one that needs to come off the callout list, is it? We already have six experienced members out of action for the next three months. Two hip replacements, one knee replacement, one coronary bypass, one cataract operation and Jim's hernia from carrying the rigging bag.'

'It's worse than that,' Gordon mumbled.

'I'll put the kettle on then.' Sharon pointed them towards the living room before going to the kitchen. The fact Gordon hadn't blurted something out already meant that it must be complicated. And why bring Howard along? Perhaps the cheque from the National Park Authority grant had bounced. But that was nothing compared to some of the crises the team had suffered in the past, such as the time they had to remove a member from the team. A young lad had taken a bit too much pleasure in doing CPR on female casualties regardless of whether they were unconscious or not. But that was years ago. Things had been calm for the last few months.

Sharon pushed her tabby cat aside with her elbow and put the tea tray on the upholstered footstool. The men were perched upright on the sofa like they had been ironed stiff. Another sign that things were bad. 'Go on then, tell me.'

'Our bank account is empty,' Gordon said, glancing at Howard.

'It's my fault,' Howard mumbled, rubbing his thin hands together like he was trying to wash them free of guilt. 'I was scammed.' He looked up at Sharon, his nostrils trembling like he'd been slapped in the face.

Howard had been the treasurer for the team for three decades since he'd discovered that heights made him vomit.

'Have you checked with the bank? Can we get it back?' Sharon asked.

'I'm on the case,' Gordon said, 'but it might take years. If ever.'

'I'm so sorry,' Howard put his head in his hands. 'It was one of those calls that claimed I had to move the money quickly. I can't believe I fell for it.'

'So how much have we lost?' Sharon thought of the effort she had put in applying for grants, organising talks at Rotary club meetings and taking collecting tins to the bank.

'About £80,000,' Gordon said with a deep sigh.

'So is that why you've come here, to ask me to raise more money?' Sharon looked out of the window. A robin sitting on the stonewall met her gaze and tilted his head as if he recognised the challenge she was facing.

'Not all of it straight away, of course, just enough for the next few months, or a year perhaps. Enough time to let us try and get our funds back,' Gordon said and looked at Howard for approval.

'So roughly £30,000?' Sharon clarified.

'Something like that. It would cover the running costs and allow us to replace any broken equipment for the next year. We would need help from the rest of the team of course.'

'So what are your suggestions?'

'Grants?' Gordon asked raising his eyebrows in the hope of a quick solution.

'Takes too long.'

'We could ask each team member to raise £1000 from family and friends?'

'You're joking,' Sharon replied. 'Apart from the most recent team members, everyone else's friends and family have already been milked dry. It's not going to work. We need to attract new donors, people who are happy to give more than a couple of quid.'

'We could do with a pet rescue, that always attracts a lot of donations. If we feature in the news - even better.'

'But how often do we have one of those? Once every two or three years at most. And don't say we should kidnap a celebrity dog and stage an accident.'

'Know of any legacies from wills coming soon?'

'Don't even go there...' Sharon sat down facing her visitors, a cup of steaming tea between her hands.

'What if we go public and say we've been scammed and desperate for funds. Would that work?'

Sharon shook her head. 'No, we'd just look incompetent. We should keep this strictly within the team.'

Howard sighed, his only contribution to the discussion.

Sharon wasn't sure if it was in response to being called incompetent or if he was relieved there wouldn't be a public announcement about it. She put her cup down and picked up her knitting. 'I think better if I keep my hands busy.'

The three of them sat in silence as the light faded outside. Gordon was about to give his apologies when Sharon cleared her throat.

'I can't think of a way forward. We'll have to approach the rest of the team for ideas.'

Gordon was sandwiched between Sharon and the team secretary Stuart in the meeting room at the mountain rescue base. Howard had been allowed to stay at home as they feared that he might collapse from the stress of having to acknowledge his error to the rest of the team.

'Thank you everyone for coming tonight despite the short notice,' Gordon addressed the room full of team members with suspicion written across their faces. The good turnout was largely due to him not having mentioned fundraising in the invite and instead gathered everyone under the impression that they would be given a new waterproof jacket, a tip he'd got from Sharon. It was largely accepted that the team consisted of people who preferred to risk their lives dangling on ropes rather than stand on a street corner shaking collecting tins. But still, it was the team's responsibility to support itself financially, with its money largely coming from donations from the public.

When everyone had been told about the unfortunate financial mistake and the poor prospects of quickly recovering the money, they set to debating ways they could replace the funds.

'We could do a raffle? Like a proper lottery or something?' someone suggested.

'To raise £30,000? What are you suggesting we have as a prize? One of the Land Rovers?' Jim blurted out.

'Please, let's not ridicule any suggestions,' Sharon urged. 'Unfortunately, lotteries are heavily regulated and a raffle will at most raise a few hundred. Let's add the suggestion to the minutes and move on.'

'Maybe we could organise an event?' someone else offered up as an idea. 'Remember the cycling challenge twenty years ago in the form of a Wensleydale pub crawl? It raised quite a lot of money for the team and lots of our members completed it too.'

'I remember that,' Jim said, 'Although, my memory is a bit hazy past the Fox and Hounds in West Witton.'

'There's no way such an event would be acceptable these days,' Sharon pointed out. 'It would go against our image of wanting to keep people safe.'

'How about organising a Skinny Dip like they do at Druridge Bay beach? They raise thousands for charity at that event,' a voice came from the back of the room.

'What? In the river Swale?' Gordon said in disbelief. 'Have you seen it recently after all the rain we've had? It would be like that time all those mannequins fell in the river. No thanks. There must be a better way.'

'What about a calendar?' Stuart suggested. He looked very pleased with his idea, no doubt envisaging himself posing in a naughty elf costume in front of a Land Rover for December.

'You mean like a naked calendar?' Gordon asked and dropped his eyebrows.

People squirmed in their seats, eyeing each other up and down.

'Well, there's the proof if it was ever needed,' Sarah said triumphantly, being one of the few team members who had voiced concerns about the narrow demographic of the team. 'If only the team had been able to attract younger members and addressed the skewed gender ratio, we could have sold quite a few.'

A quick look around the room confirmed that it had been a futile proposal. It was doubtful that even the member's own families would be willing to part with cash to get their hands on a calendar, never mind a stranger.

The room smelled of pessimism as people stared at their feet unable to think of any new fundraising ideas that wouldn't immediately be dismissed.

Gordon cleared his throat. 'I fear we have tough times ahead as we try to build up the funds using our regular channels of fundraising. What we'd need is something to hit the national news. Something totally out of the ordinary that will make people all over the country donate to us. Such as an enormously complicated and drawn-out rescue with high stakes for everyone involved.

'You mean like an underground rescue?' Jim asked.

'Exactly.'

That was the moment people realised that not a single one of the team's keen cavers was present in the room.

'Has anyone seen any of the underground people since their party in Canoodle Pot yesterday?' Gordon asked with a brewing feeling of unease in his stomach. 'No?' It was now Sunday evening. If some of them were still too hungover to attend the meeting, that wouldn't have surprised him. But all of them?

Sarah got to her feet and disappeared out of the room, only to reappear thirty seconds later. 'The underground store is empty. There's not a single piece of rescue kit left. They must still be down the cave.'

For a few minutes, the room was silent while people processed the challenge facing them. Not only had few of them attended more than the minimum number of underground rescue training sessions, but there was no specialised equipment left for them to use. It wouldn't be long until the alarm would be raised and all hell would break loose. This was going national whether they wanted it or not. A text message broke the silence. Gordon looked at his phone and then at the people in the room. 'It's the police. Someone has enquired why there are over a hundred cars abandoned in the middle of nowhere. The police have just asked me if I know anything about it.'

'I'll call the catering in,' Jim announced. 'Canoodle Pot, did you say?'

Gordon nodded and scanned the room. 'Looks like we got what we wished for.'

'What *you* wished for,' Stuart muttered.

'I suggest you all go home and get ready. I'll contact the neighbouring teams for help. This rescue could go on for days. Normally, I'd say we should keep media out of it, but this time, Sharon, you run with it.' Gordon stood up looking at the wide-eyed team members in front of him. 'What are you all waiting for? Let's go.'

Three weeks later…
'126,256 pounds and 12 pence. Not bad at all. And that's after we split the donations with the other teams. After all, they did most of the rescuing,' Sharon replied when Gordon asked her what was currently in the team's bank account.

'Does that include the £80 000 that the bank recovered from the Cayman Islands?'

'No, that will be repaid to us next week,' Howard replied with a faint smile across his lips.

They were sitting in front of the woodburning stove in Sharon's living room. Gordon's bruises were finally beginning to fade. He'd never been at the front face of an underground rescue before and his body had taken a battering. Howard was unbleamished, having neither got wet nor had to dangle off a rope. Sharon's cat was purring on his lap.

'It's a bit of a shame though,' Gordon started, 'that £120,000 of it is earmarked for supporting underground rescues. It would have been nice to get the team some new jackets.'

'Craig said he'd been approached by Pixar about letting them have the movie rights for his ordeal,' Sharon said as she poured hot black tea into the three porcelain cups on the tray balanced on the footstool.

'Pixar? Don't they do animated children's films?' Gordon asked.

'Yes. Craig's part will be played by a cartoon mole with claustrophobia. He's said he'll donate the money from it to the team since he doesn't want his name associated with it in any way.'

'And another piece of good news!' Gordon announced sitting up straight. 'The number of applications to join the team is up by a factor of ten. You'll be pleased to know fundraising skills will be taken into account when choosing which ones to put forward.'

'That's great. We'll need it. I heard that one of the Land Rovers is about to die on us.' Sharon gave Gordon a stern look. 'Just ensure the selection weekend doesn't include a wet t-shirt competition, will you?'

'No worries, I'll oversee it myself.'

'So what are the underground people going to spend all their money on? Not more rum I hope?' Sharon asked.

'No, they're drawing up plans for reconfiguring the underground store,' Gordon admitted.

'What? An underground store of the underground store of the underground store?'

'Not quite. They want to relocate it to Canoodle Pot. They claim the location is closer to where we get our underground callouts. Also, during the two weeks they were trapped, they created an underground hub within the cave system where they could train and hang out. In any case, all their equipment is still down there.' Gordon stood up and placed his empty tea cup on the tray. Howard, sensing it was time to leave, followed suit.

'Could be controversial with the rest of the team?' Sharon suggested.

'Don't I know it! I'm not looking forward to next week's committee meeting.'

Sharon saw Gordon and Howard out. The air was unseasonally cold, frost sparkling on the frozen grass in the weak sunshine. As the two men walked away a few large snowflakes drifted from the sky. She looked at them settling on the garden path in front of her door. The hills in the distance already had a dusting of snow. Today might be a good day to ski up Great Shunner Fell and empty the collecting tin that she'd wedged into a gap between two rocks at the stone shelter, just in case any walkers had felt generous after reaching the summit.

Year 2053

A knock on the door woke Gordon from his second nap of the day. At first, he thought it might have been part of a lifelong recurring dream in which he locks himself in a toilet cubicle to avoid a trombone lesson, but then he heard it again, a soft *tap, tap, tap*. He failed to recall the last time anyone had dropped in unannounced. Most things these days were predicted by artificial intelligence or scheduled in advance to prevent people from being subjected to surprises.

Gordon knocked over a cup of cold tea while fumbling for his phone under old copies of Angling Times on the coffee table. The retina scanner would soon identify who had come to visit. He flicked back and forth between the screens until he found his doorbell app. When he finally got it launched, it only displayed the menu bar above a black screen. He jabbed his stubby finger repeatedly at his phone, but the face of his visitor refused to appear.

If his smart door had classed whoever was standing on the other side as safe based on sufficient citizen points or lack of a criminal record, he could have used a simple voice command to let them in. Another knock on the door made Gordon's chest fill with fear. Someone was outside. Someone who hadn't messaged him in advance. Someone who had disabled his surveillance camera. Common sense told him to press his alarm button to call out a police drone, but old habits got the better of him. In the first seventy years of his life, he couldn't ever remember locking his front door. Why would he suddenly require the government to vet his visitors before he welcomed them into his home?

Gordon was in his late nineties but moved smoothly thanks to the 'muscular' treatments offered to anyone over sixty. Half an hour of mild electric shocks twice a week was enough to retain his less-than-impressive physique that allowed him to live independently. That and the various robots and sensors that everyone now took for granted. Technology was the main caregiver for both old and young, and the system worked if you didn't venture too far from home, or indeed, let in malevolent strangers.

Gordon opened the door a few centimetres, enough to catch a glimpse of his visitor before the low sun hit the back of his eyes. He sneezed, letting the door fling wide open while the cold air sailed through his merino wool pyjamas. If anyone was after a vulnerable target, he was it. Shielding his eyes, he made out a slim man in dark blue ski pants and an unfashionable Gore-Tex jacket rarely spotted in public in the last couple of decades. He was surprised to see the lined face of his mountain rescue colleague, Keith, who he hadn't seen for a month or two.

Gordon was about to greet him when Keith held a finger to his lips and handed him a crumpled piece of paper. Wide-eyed, Gordon unfolded the note.

Fuck it. I'm going up Shunner.
Jim

Twenty-five years ago, going up Shunner would have been nothing unusual. On a day with a clear blue sky, with a fresh dusting of snow and no wind, there would have been at least a dozen cross-country skiers shuffling up to the top of Great Shunner Fell, only to risk breaking legs and impaling their abdomens going down the bumpy slope. The dangers were many but laughter would echo across the moors, and bruises were paraded in the pub while enjoying an après ski beer.

Twenty years ago, after a spate of lawsuits by injured outdoor enthusiasts against the landowners, anyone venturing out on the hills was made to comply with a rash of regulations, including wearing a helmet and registering your route two weeks in advance, along with signing a disclaimer.

Fifteen years ago, skiing and climbing had been banned. Special surveillance drones tracked any hikers based on their smartphone locations to keep them safe in the great outdoors, while also being able to monitor any breaches of rules. The drones became ever more zealous and would raise the alarm if people stepped off the footpath or peed behind a stonewall. A raised alarm, however innocent, would result in a deduction of citizen points and higher insurance premiums.

Ten years ago, venturing into the hills was made illegal since the monitoring costs were deemed unaffordable. By this time, risk-taking was so socially unacceptable that the ban went largely unnoticed. These days most of the people spotted on the hills were either suicidal or suffered from dementia.

Keith kept his finger across his lips and waved for Gordon to join him in the pristine snow that covered the path up to the door. Gordon held up his hand to signal that he needed a minute. He'd discovered a glitch in his smart watch that meant that as long as he turned the shower on, he could take it off without it reporting a lack of detectable heartbeat to the care company. He'd made use of it several times to go fly fishing to prevent his watch from thinking he'd fallen in the river and alerting the fire brigade. Like all the other gadgets in his house, it sent a constant stream of information to keep him safe and minimise his burden on society. Even his fridge grassed him up from time to time when it detected he'd bought too much cheese and not enough vegetables.

Gordon followed Keith around the back of the house and into the snow-covered greenhouse at the bottom of the garden.

'No gadgets?' Keith asked, looking at shrivelled tomato plants sticking out of dried-out grow-bags.

'No, for once I remembered to disconnect the automatic watering unit before the first frost.' Gordon read the note again and handed it back to Keith. 'Any idea when he left?'

'An hour ago, maybe two. His footprints head straight for the hill.' Keith grimaced.

'You're thinking what I'm thinking?'

'I'm afraid so,' Keith replied as he put the note back in his pocket.

Gordon knew that if he was spotted heading out on the fells in the snow, even for the most well-intentioned reason, it would only mean one thing to the algorithms: he'd lost his marbles. He'd have to spend the rest of his life in a care home where they wouldn't let him out of sight. His heart made a few erratic jumps inside his chest as he looked at the pond his wife dug the year before she died. He still had to feed Hector, the koi carp, who seemed determined to outlive both of them. But Gordon knew what they had to do. 'We've got no time to lose.'

Ten minutes later, they pulled open Keith's sagging garage doors, creating half-moons in the snow. Old ropes, bundles of aluminium caving ladders and a few stretchers lay stacked on wooden shelves inside the gloomy space. Rubber bags containing inflatable boats were stacked along the walls with yellow and black paddles piled on top. Every piece of equipment was covered in a thick layer of dust.

'Hey, I remember these!' Gordon said as he lifted the lid off a plastic box full of head torches. 'I had no idea you managed to salvage this much kit.'

Fourteen years earlier, the country's mountain rescue organisations had dissolved. The drop in hikers combined with the development of recovery drones, able to find and transport any casualties, meant that there was no longer any need for voluntary organisations to be on continuous standby. The Swaledale team had been told to dispose of the kit responsibly to avoid encouraging people to use it. Keith, the team's equipment officer, had clearly interpreted this as permission to take it all home.

They pulled the two halves of a heavy stretcher from a shelf. Gordon balanced the top half on the bottom half, relishing the feel of the cold stainless steel runners fitted to the stretcher's underside. Keith twiddled with the complicated fasteners to join the halves together. Memories from the team's rescues flooded in from long-forgotten corners of his mind. The occasional panic, the sometimes inappropriate jokes, but always the privilege to help an injured person, to bring them to safety and hand them over to experienced health professionals. Now and again, the casualty's poor judgement or insufficient preparation had contributed to their misadventure but mostly it was just bad luck. It was weird how, in the current society, bad luck was almost non-existent; it had effectively been legislated away.

'Cas bag?' Gordon asked.

'Sure.' Keith spun around on his heels and picked up a soft red bag that would offer warmth and comfort to a casualty during the evacuation. They strapped it onto the stretcher. 'Anything else?'

'Are those what I think they are?' Gordon pointed to a corner of the garage. He remembered the long-lasting discussion in the rescue team committee meeting after someone suggested after a particularly snowy winter that the team should issue every member a pair of cross-country skis. They had eventually purchased a couple of sets for evaluation that, by the looks of it, had never been unwrapped.

'Looks like they'll finally come in handy!' Keith announced and grinned. In his eagerness to collect the skis, he knocked a small cardboard box off a shelf and dozens of red beanies with big bobbles tumbled to the floor.

'No way!' Gordon shouted. 'I can't believe it. I thought we decided not to get them on the basis that they wouldn't fit under our helmets.'

Keith looked up and blushed. 'Craig ordered them without telling anyone. Arrived a week before we were disbanded. Removable bobbles. Never got the chance to hand them out.'

Gordon opened a packet and pulled a hat over his ears. 'Let's go.'

They set off towards Great Shunner Fell, which was more of a lump covered in bogs and coarse grass than a real mountain. Still, at just over 700 metres it seemed to tower over the village. They took turns pulling the stretcher, stopping regularly to hack off chunks of compacted snow stuck to the underside of their skis. Soft white hills queued up as far as the eye could see, the roads standing out as black lines in the valley bottoms. Decades earlier, they had often combed the fell for missing people in dense fog while the wind peppered their faces with tiny icicles. Today though, the conditions were perfect.

'I never thought I'd get up here again,' Gordon said, plumes of misty breath guiding his words into the air.

'Nice, isn't it?'

In the far distance, a drone was hovering like an angry bumblebee above a car that had pulled into a layby near a once popular beauty spot. The doors didn't open and soon the car continued its journey.

Gordon froze. The drone was heading towards them.

'It might have picked us up on the infrared,' Keith shouted. 'Let's pretend we're sheep.'

They dropped on all fours, tilting their heads down like they were looking for grass to chomp on.

'You sure this will work?' Gordon asked.

'It'll only detect heat from our faces. The rest is too cold, too much insulation, just like sheep. Just keep your head down.'

The buzzing noise hovered above them for a few seconds before it sped off into the distance, having picked up the movement from a car on the road below.

When Gordon and Keith got close to the top, they fell silent, worrying about what state Jim would be in when they found him. There was only one set of footprints leading up the hill. He hadn't come back down, at least not by the same route.

Jim had taken the changes in society harder than most, especially when the government introduced a ban on alcohol after pressure from healthcare professionals and religious groups. He had never taken to the digital transformation that had made life for everyone else less burdensome and didn't even own a smartphone. Instead, he had fought the system and failed. His citizen score was close to zero which meant that anyone detected in his presence risked points being deducted from their own score. He'd become an outcast.

When Gordon had conquered the final incline to reach the top, he saw the familiar scrawny silhouette of his old friend sitting in the snow, his upper body leaning forward and his arms stretched like he was saying his last prayer.

'Jim! Are you okay?' Gordon tripped over his skis in his hurry to get close to his friend and ended up sprawled on his stomach, ski poles sticking out from beneath him.

'Gordon. Impeccable timing,' came the response.

Jim didn't sound distressed, relieved or annoyed. He sounded casual, borderline happy. Gordon pushed himself to a seated position and unfastened the narrow cross-country skis from his boots. He saw that Jim wasn't praying but instead fighting with a box buried in the frozen ground.

'Are you alright?' Gordon asked as he watched his former mountain rescue colleague pull hard at the dented lid, trying to flip it open.

A crack sounded when the lid gave way and Jim looked up. 'Why wouldn't I be?'

'Your note.'

At that moment they were joined by Keith who looked relieved to find Jim not just alive but in a cheerful mood.

'Remember this?' Jim asked and pointed to the box. 'Richard buried it in the summer of 2017 for us to enjoy during the following winter. We thought he'd gone mad. The weather never was pleasant enough to crack it open.'

Gordon had forgotten all about it and blushed thinking of the effort that had gone into transporting it up the mountain.

In the box lay a couple of bottles of mulled wine, their labels partly eaten by slugs, together with a dozen paper cups and a camping stove. Jim shook the metal canister. 'Looks like the fuel has evaporated. Never mind. We'll drink it cold.'

A few metres behind them were a couple of stonewalls positioned at an angle to provide shelter from the wind. The men, each holding a cup of mulled wine, trudged through the snow and sat down on top of the stretcher with their backs against the stonewall looking out over the valley below. On lower ground, the snow had melted to reveal pale green grass. The hills, white and pure, showed not a single soul out enjoying themselves.

'Nobody knows we're here, right?' Gordon said.

'Or what we're doing,' Jim added.

'I could get used to this,' Keith chimed in.

They didn't say much else, each sipping the sweet liquid that had more than a hint of vinegar, while taking in the view. Memories of past adventures flooded their minds and a feeling of well-being filled their hearts. After fifteen minutes, the cold was nipping at their hands and feet.

'Same time next week?' Jim asked. 'There's another bottle in the box.'

The other two nodded.

'Which reminds me,' Keith said. 'I've got the contents of the underground store in my garage. Quite a few bottles of rum left if I remember correctly.'

'Same time every week then,' Jim replied, his broad smile revealing several missing teeth.

They washed their cups out with snow and returned them to the box.

Jim glanced at his friends' skis. 'I suppose I'll use the stretcher to get down, or I won't keep up with you lot.'

They lined up on the edge of the hill and looked down the treacherous descent that was interspersed with boggy ruts and stone boulders sticking out of the uneven snow cover.

'Let's hope luck is on our side!' Gordon shouted as they pushed off. Frightened grouse lept in the air as the threesome hurtled down the hill laughing louder than they had done in years.

Dear Mountain Rescue…

Dear Mountain Rescue Team,

I just want to thank you for coming to my assistance last week when I collapsed in the cottage I was staying in. It's the first time something like this has happened to me and I can't tell you how grateful I am that someone was able to help.

Today my friends visited me in the hospital and told me how I had fainted after taking a bite out of an apple. I don't remember any of it, as you can imagine! They said the paramedics had called you when they saw the steep and rocky track to the cottage.

My friends mentioned how delighted they were to have been asked to help carry the stretcher down to the road. Not an easy task, I can imagine, due to their short stature, so no wonder you dropped me! My friends aren't sure if it was the impact with the ground or the mouth-to-mouth from the handsome chap in your team that made me regain consciousness. Just in case it was the latter, please give him my sincere thanks.

Thanks again to all of you from me and my friends,
Snowwhite, Doc, Happy, Grumpy, Sleepy, Dopey, Bashful and Sneezy

PS. My stepmother is coming to visit this afternoon and I can't wait to tell her all about it!

*

Dear Mountain Rescue,
I am writing to you to ask for your help. I'm trying to track down my sister Heather Burke. The last time I heard from her was three months ago. The police have said there is nothing else that they can do. Her flat was empty when they went to check.
Her not telling me her new address is out of character. She also seemed happily settled in her last place and wanted to introduce me to a guy she was seeing. The last time I spoke to her she said something about having to go and buy a caving suit. I know this is grasping for straws, but since you guys go underground a lot as part of your training and rescues, could you keep your ears to the ground for any news?

Many thanks,

Nigel Burke

*

Dear Keith,

Thank you for your enquiry regarding detachable bobbles for bobble hats. I am happy to say that we, The Specialist Bobble Hat Company, could provide these to you in the colour you requested. Unfortunately, we do not keep this particular type in stock so they would have to be shipped from our supplier in India. The minimum quantity is 500 and the extra cost compared to a regular bobble hat is £2 per item. Please let us know if you wish to place an order and for how many.

Yours,
Frankie Ansari

*

Interviewer: Elaine Brookes, Coroner's officer (EB)
Interviewee: Gordon Cutter, MR Chair
Date and time: January 5th 2023 13:00
Location: Scottish Fatalities Investigation Unit (SFIU), Glasgow

[1:20:31 into recording]

EB: Were you worried?

GC: Was I worried? Of course I was. I knew Colin had had a rough time, even though he never talked about it. He wasn't a particularly cheerful person at the best of times. And that morning? We were all a bit pissed off, to be honest. A stretcher-carry, sure, you'd be home in a couple of hours. But a search? We knew Christmas Day was ruined. Colin didn't seem any angrier than anyone else though. Well, I was wrong, wasn't I? God, was I wrong… At the time, I thought he was genuinely worried about Martin, the misper. We were all convinced it was a great idea, him going to stay at Colin's place. [Deep sigh].

EB: What did you do after you got the phone call from Martin's wife?

GC: I called Colin straight away, but he didn't answer. Tried both mobile and landline. But something didn't feel right, so I drove over to Colin's house to check.

EB: What time?

GC: Just before noon, Boxing Day.

EB: And wha–

GC: I was too late. They… they were both… Can you switch that off, please? I need a minute.

[End of recorded material]

*

Dear Mountain Rescue,

I attended the Open Day you did last year with my chihuahua Bruce and, despite him doing really well, we haven't had an invitation to join the team yet. I understand you predominantly use border collies as search dogs, but I'd like to remind you that any reputable organisation values diversity amongst their members and I feel this should also include your search dogs. Admittedly he is not as fast as a collie, due to his short legs, but he sniffs more thoroughly than any other dog I've come across, so I'm sure he'd be a great asset to your team.

I look forward to hearing from you soon.

Sophie Mills

*

Dear Mountain Rescue,

I would like to express my sincere gratitude for coming to rescue my daughter's spaniel Ruby when she fell into a pothole whilst in my care. I am so sorry for having called you out so early in the morning as I'm sure you were all very busy or in need of a rest.

I just want to say how impressed I was, not only with the quick response time, but also with how you made it all happen even though I was in such a state and not able to contribute in any shape or form. I now realise what an asset the mountain rescue team is to everyone, unlucky or foolish, who finds themselves in need of help for whatever reason. To know that a team of well-trained and selfless men and women can come to anyone's rescue, anywhere at any time is a comforting thought.

I know you work as a team and that every team member contributes to your success, but I would particularly like to thank the lady (I'm very sorry that I didn't catch her name) who thanks to her petite stature and immense bravery was able to retrieve Ruby from the deep hole. I was going to enclose a donation but the amount I would have been able to give you would have been insultingly low due to my current circumstances. Instead, I have decided to include you as a beneficiary in my will and in due course (unfortunately for me, not very long) a more substantiation contribution will come your way.

Thank you ever so much and keep up your good work,

Hugh Bramsworth

Acknowledgements

My deepest gratitude goes to Sarah, a fellow student on my masters degree in creative writing, whose insightful suggestions, honest opinions and never-ending willingness to read my stories again and again made me carry on writing until I had enough for a complete book.

I am indebted to my trusted proof-readers Astrid McIntyre, Richard Denny, Jane Beaumont and Jill Armstrong, who helped me spot all my mistakes and offer suggestions for improvements.

I would also like to thank members from the Swaledale Mountain and Cave Rescue Team such as Tim Rothwell, Bob Southwell, Adam Bradley, Rich Clarke and most of all Pete Roe, for providing inspiration and information to make these stories come alive.

About the Author

Emmy Hoyes was born in Sweden but now lives in the Yorkshire Dales with her dog Daphne. She joined the Swaledale Mountain Rescue Team in 2018 and completed a master's degree in creative writing with the Open University in 2023.

If you enjoyed these stories you will also like her previously published trilogy, featuring unlikely heroes and humorous calamities.

His Favourite Hole
Lost Baggage
The Pigeon Trap

Printed in Great Britain
by Amazon